Dedicated to Andy, the best father-in-law

I became insane, with long intervals of horrible sanity —
Edgar Allan Poe

COAL HOUSE

W.S. Barton

Rudling House Publishing Limited,
Kemp House, 152 City Road, London EC1V 2NX

Published in the UK in 2015 by Rudling House.
A CIP catalogue record for this book is available
from the British Library

ISBN 978-1-910957-00-4

Front cover image by Ashley Temple
www.ashleytemple.co.uk
Cover and typeset by Karen Ronan
www.coversbykaren.com

RH

www.rudlinghouse.com

Chapter One
Clara

OF COURSE there was some excitement about us on the day. I had never even set foot in an auction room let alone participated in the bidding in one and so the prospect of doing so was one that was filled with excitement and anticipation and unknowing. Clara and I had an idea of what we wanted... well, in truth, I knew what *I* wanted. I wanted a house like the one my grandparents had had in North London, a terraced part of a community we could grow into and become a part of. A wider family.

That feeling had grown ever since Clara's dear mother, June, had passed away the previous year. The sadness was matched by the isolation; we were both only children, young children born to parents in older age. We were war babies — or war children — our fathers had both fought in the First World War and we were both always told stories of how the fragility of life, and seeing death, had changed their outlooks on life. Having been more than happy to spend their lives as couples without children, they changed their mind. We were both old enough to experience the terror of the Second World War. It almost seemed a matter of fate that Clara and I would be drawn to each other, as if it were some contrived path that had already been drawn.

It wasn't until I was 23 and Clara was 21 that we met, working at a newspaper press. Clara was a dreamer, a blonde haired whirlwind of sass that stormed into my life and I, well... Let's just say I found it hard to concentrate. That was certainly the case with Clara around and when she left the printers to pursue a career in fashion as a designer and tailor I grew disillusioned with my own path, so ended up with a number of different careers, none of them lasting more than a few months.

Thankfully my relationship with Clara had more longevity; I think we saw a lot of our parents in each other. Clara was certainly her mother's daughter, with ambition and hope, and an eye for things that I could never see. I was growing into my own father, increasingly embittered by the life I felt I had been dealt, to be occasionally shot back into the self awareness that I was doing it to myself.

Growing up, I'd always thought that Dad's mutterings were ones that had a great deal of truth to them — that the Man, whoever he was, was responsible for his lack of progression or at least his own sense of achievement. It was only when I turned thirty and looked at re-evaluating where I'd come from and where I was that I realised I had emulated Dad's path prior to him having to go to War. He had passed by then so I was unable to ask him if that was the case, if it was a matter of he himself holding him back rather than external forces. Even if he'd been around when I had my moment of awakening, I don't know if I'd have had the guts to have confronted him with what I felt was the truth. Mum, God bless her, knew all too well. She tried to over-compensate with the push of a mother's belief, sending me to Grammar School. I was educated but disillusioned, but not disillusioned enough to take a stand. That frustrated me too. What was my purpose? My early mid-life crisis was stopped in its tracks by June's passing. My parents had both passed a little earlier and I felt that I had dealt with it well. I had been close to them, and naturally for a time, I had been heartbroken, but I did not dwell as much as I thought I might. I had no prior experience with grief. Both sets of my grandparents had died before I was born, apart from my grandmother on my mother's side, but she died when I was a baby and I sadly had no memory of having known her at all. For some reason, I felt more affected when Clara's parents died. Maybe it was because we were left alone. Isolation had always been something that intrigued me and scared me in a sense because, growing up as I had, I had never felt it. In London, we were never far away from anyone.

June had left a rather large inheritance in addition to the house she and Clara's dad, Frank, had lived in; she never moved out of there despite our insistence that she should live with us. Clara felt she died of a broken heart — she may have had a point as it was only fourteen months after Frank had passed. I could understand, appreciate and respect June's decision to remain where she was, because Clara and I had moved into my old home when we inherited it.

Clara had spent so much time trying to convince June to move that I think, in the end, she herself had grown to believe the reasons she was giving. There was too much emotional attachment, it wasn't healthy to dwell. So when it came to dealing with the goods and possessions that became my responsibility as it was something that Clara had developed a coldness towards; I knew that it was borne out of hurt, and a refusal to accept what had happened.

Those two polarising reactions to grief provided a contrast but I grew to believe that June's way was the healthier. To dwell wasn't the most advancing of approaches but it was probably better than to refuse to deal with it at all. I saw June as a step further in the process. In the end, who is to know and who is to be told what is right? June took her way to the grave and she seemed quite content to do so.

Still, her passing brought upon a huge change in the dynamic of the relationship between Clara and I. Unsurprisingly, Clara sold the house and was sat on a windfall of money that enabled her to quit her job as someone else's designer and begin to work for herself. For the longest time, she urged me to quit my own job as a delivery driver, saying I could work with her and we could spend more time together. I was suffering my own grief and although I could later rationalise my response as illogical, I resisted on the grounds that I couldn't bear either of us to be as broken hearted as we sometimes saw June, or my own mother, in their weaker moments. Distance would do us good. Of course, I never told Clara that, but she knew. She would often question me directly on it but I insisted that I loved my own work. On the first anniversary of June's passing I finally admitted to myself, and to Clara, openly that what I really wanted was to spend more time with my wife. We had been given a freedom, a freedom which was at first terrifying, but one that should have been liberating in the truest sense of the term.

We sat down and tried to think of what would be the best thing for us to do in order to best make the use of Clara's artistic and creative flair, my history of odd-jobs and contacts I'd built up, and the financial freedom we now had and the natural solution was to move into property development and real estate.

When it came to buying our first property I shared all of Clara's excitement but I was so set on the idea of creating a home like the ones we had lived in, for others to benefit from. Clara, on the other hand, was quite taken by the potential to design a home for a young professional, the type which I suspected she had often wished to be. I acquiesced to her wishes for she was the one with the nous and we acquired a two bedroom apartment in Westminster after an auction which was keenly contested between us and two other parties.

I must confess that I got quite the thrill from the process, the greatest being observing the life in Clara's eyes as we drew closer to what we felt was the conclusion; it was worth bidding a little over what we had budgeted to see her so full of excitement again.

It took a little over eight months for Clara to get things how she wanted; anyone else might have taken half the time for a similar result but in the things she had control over, she was a definite perfectionist and it was inspiring in its own way to observe the passion she held for her craft. I am biased of course but I quickly became one with the opinion that she was a master of it — though as time went on, I couldn't help but think that she had developed such a love for what she was doing that it had moved away from the original concept of us spending more time together.

That feeling was accentuated by the relationship she seemed to develop with these contained walls, this empty shell that was simply a percentage of someone else's property. As the project drew nearer to completion I sensed a longing for the life she had begun to imagine herself living there.

I was relieved, then, when the time came to sell — it had always been our intention although Clara's resistance wavered as we waded through the politics of estate agents and so forth. The clinical nature of the way everyone took their slice of the pie and the way it didn't seem to reflect Clara's personal touch left her somewhat disenchanted with the experience and that most certainly resonated in our following projects. Our second was another apartment in central London as Clara desperately tried to recreate what she had done before, but we both knew it was a vain attempt to relive a 'first love'.

We made a greater profit from that apartment — far from make Clara happy, it made her question her own eye and feeling. As if the difference was a personal assessment of the work she had done rather than a cold and frank representation of the property market. I tried to re-assure her that in anybody's terms, she had been a success, and that is what she ought to be proud of, but — and this was one of the things I loved so tremendously of her — she saw value not in monetary terms but the effort and love with which something was treated.

One summer evening, shortly after the sale of the second property, we went for a stroll around the lake in Waterlow Park, near to where we had grown up, and, probably unbeknown to us (or at least, we liked to romantically pretend this was the case) spent many times near each other without even knowing.

'Finn?' asked Clara, with a purpose and hope of persuasion in her voice.

'Yes darling?'

'I think I would quite like to make a home here again. You know, like you wanted.'

If it was music to my ears at the time I only wish I had learned my lesson in my observations and trusted my own judgement. It was never to be plain sailing, never to be the rosy scenario I and she anticipated. Clara had convinced herself that she could buy her mother's house back but when it wasn't for sale she looked for another on the same street, as close to the same dimensions and layout as she could. None were available, and so she waited until one became so. We tried with the best of intentions but the whole process was a disaster. Clara went as far as she felt she reasonably could, saturating the house with reminders of the way she remembered it, or, at least, the way she remembered the one she had grown up in.

Needless to say, a journey back in time thirty years was not one that was going to prove too endearing to modern eyes, especially when that journey was through the specific eyes to the childhood of another. She had been so headstrong and dedicated to the idea that she was particularly crestfallen when, more than halfway through, she began to realise that it wasn't right. That much was reflecting in the selling process, and we lost a considerable amount of money.

We both had our own respective moments of reflection and I admit that I often thought if Clara's involved her life and future with me. Whether she'd made the right choice. We had made decisions together for what we felt were the purest of reasons in terms of fulfillment both for our relationship and careers and the setback, being such a personal one for both of us, seemed a significant moment.

Chapter Two
The Percys

IT HAD been a testing time to say the least and it was with that in mind that I decided to surprise Clara with a long weekend break for our seventh wedding anniversary. I remembered how once, we had worked with somebody with a delightfully melodic accent who would speak fondly of the place from where he came and learned that he was from North Wales. It had interested me to at least explore a little of my own and I learned that there were some getaways that promised breathtaking scenery and fresh air and it sounded divine.

I found a cottage in a small village near Llandudno, a bed and breakfast away from everything but each other, with the hope that our life minus the distractions could be given a new focus. I was so dearly in love with Clara and couldn't bear for us to be apart and the thought that she may not feel the same anymore had plagued me so much that I kept it quiet from her.

My intentions were as honest and true as any 'anniversary' surprise might be but my motivation was one that she was not privy to. It was my hope that such a break would be sufficient to silence my inner doubts. I had felt a distance at times, which

I had attributed to our troubles in losing both sets of parents in a relatively quick space of time and then suffering some financial hardship as well as that disillusion which most people feel when they reach a milestone in their life.

If there was any substance to my thoughts, then, Clara was giving her best poker face. She had not treated me any differently and there had been all the moments of... tenderness, that any loving marriage enjoys. On my better days I would scold and ridicule myself for even thinking anything was wrong and it was one of those better days when we boarded our train from Euston Station north through towns, cities and hamlets, encountering a number of changes until we finally reached our destination of Aberaernavon.

The journey, despite its length, was quite jovial, with Clara looking forward to the time away and hoping to recapture some kind of excitement in the quaint architecture one often finds as commonplace in smaller towns not yet acquainted with the industry of the Capital. Despite the late hour we arrived, we were delighted to discover upon our arrival that Aberaernavon was as quaint and populated with such architecture as we had hoped and discussed at some length on the journey. We caught a taxi from outside the station but it was a distance we easily could have walked to our destination without too much trouble.

Accounting for late arrivals due to the scarcity of the trains, the Percy Arms remained open so we could check into our room. We were greeted by the landlord, to my mind a stereotypical post- middle-aged Northerner, with a swelled belly and reddened cheeks just about visible over the dark grey beard which covered the majority of his face. I imagined he would be employed as the local Santa Claus in just over a months' time, be it for a grotto or store. He was certainly a welcoming fellow for weary travelers.

'Hello, name's Hector Percy, and you must be Clara,' he said, offering his hand to me. 'Only joking!' he continued with a roar of laughter, 'Come on in, come on in. Now we've still got the oven on so what can we do for you... hot food, a sandwich? I imagine after all that travel you must have worked up quite a thirst. What will it be, a whisky, a beer? Wine?' He was as hospitable as garrulous, it seemed. His accent was strong but I could tell he was trying to tone it down — it was, too, the first opportunity we'd had in Wales to really hear it, aside from three or four words with the cab driver.

'A sandwich would be great, thank you Mr Percy,' I replied, before nudging my head towards Clara.

'Yes, a sandwich would be lovely', she agreed.

We stayed up rather late, introducing ourselves and getting to know Hector and his wife Lillian. Hector had inherited the pub he ran and it was named after his Grandfather, who had built it. As time went on, of course, they became more relaxed and it did become a little more difficult to understand them, so much time was spent with them repeating themselves a little slower. Still, it was wonderful to listen to, and when Hector and Lillian would speak to each other, they would generally do so in Welsh, before Lillian would steer the conversation back into our mutual language. Although not boastful of owning what appeared to be the primary venue for socialising in the area, Hector was nonetheless very proud and it struck me that he found the opportunity to speak to somebody new very welcome. For that matter, so did we, and it was only when our body clocks seemed to force the matter that we all called it a night and headed for bed.

Chapter Three
The Auction

WE AWOKE rather groggily and with sore heads. It was impossible to determine if that was due to the alcohol consumed or the lack of sleep but our more pressing concern was that we may have disturbed other guests — seemingly, our respect for others was disregarded upon arrival, and with this hypothetical remorse hanging over us I began to question what kind of first impression I might have made to our generous hosts.

Thankfully as we made our way down for breakfast it appeared that we had disturbed nobody, for nobody else was there — that was, except for Mr and Mrs Percy, who were sat in the same seats as the previous night, as if they hadn't moved, save for the content of their drinks.

We exchanged pleasantries — not quite as boisterous as the previous evening — although Lillian was particularly helpful and forthcoming with advice on what to do and see in the local area and Hector was no less hospitable than we had already become accustomed to.

On Lillian's advice we decided to go for a walk up the hills and were rewarded for doing so, for the views were breathtaking. The village itself was charming and full of character and the climb was nothing unexpected. It was a most welcome opportunity to be with Clara in nothing but the elements, away from the interrupting sounds and lights of the big city. After walking and climbing for a good hour with ambitions of reaching the very top of the hill, we scaled back our expectations and settled on a point that still hadn't been easy to reach. Looking upon the vast scenery it was refreshing to see how much of it hadn't been touched by the human hand, or, at least, appeared to be that way, to our left. To our right, we saw the opposite, hills and valleys for miles, disrupted towards the edge of the coast by disused mines which had obviously been dormant for so many years that they carried their own charm. It was there where I felt enough bravado — or foolishness — to broach the subject that had been on my mind for quite some time.

'I do love you, Clara,' I said.

'And I you,' she replied, earnestly but with more than a hint of curiosity.

'Do you... I wonder sometimes if I'm enough. I wonder if you look at what you are and what you could have been.'

'Do *you*?'

I didn't need any time to think it over. For a second I was appalled she had asked.

'Good God, no... I mean... no,' I said, incredulously, but instantly questioning my own poser in return.

Understandably there was an awkward silence between us.

It was broken by an unexpected direction.

'Finn, I don't want children... I know you do. I guess that's why we're out here rediscovering our love for one another in all of this isolation... and I love you so much. So much. But I don't want children.'

I was taken aback. Partly because it was one of the last answers I'd expected. Also because that was a statement that was delivered so matter of fact it couldn't do anything other than pierce me. I had long suspected that it was the case — neither of us were getting any younger was a factor but the timing of the tragic events of Clara's life was another that I had hoped had only temporarily caused her to seek solace elsewhere. Some seek it in the arms of another, and I had always considered my wife to be of a stronger character than that.

Yet I had concluded to myself that her unwillingness to discuss the matter of having children — though, I have to admit, it was a topic not often raised by myself — was but simply a brief moment in our lives together. I had never thought to rule it out completely and, possibly in my naivety, had always thought it was an eventuality.

To say I was stunned by what I considered to be a revelation was an understatement yet it clearly didn't seem to feel like it was a comment that should have been news. I should have known. Did I not know my wife? Who was the person I was seeing? Had she changed so much in the last few years? And if so, who could really blame her? I wasn't the same person that I was, the same man that she had met, and she knew and understood it, and we had grown together, or so I had thought. The matter of children was something that had never been raised because everything else was happening. It never felt like the right time, but it always felt as if there would have been a time. Maybe Clara did feel like that once.

Still, with each passing day and each trivial life event taking precedence over the urgency of having children, I couldn't help but think that she had reached a decision by herself. Whatever it was, it was too much for me to comprehend and give a fair and rational answer to on the spur of the moment.

'Ok'.

I put my arm around her shoulders and drew her closer as we gazed over the hills down into the village. I was both relieved that we seemed to be okay with each other, and heartbroken about the news I had received. I attempted to contrive & impose some positivity onto the conversation.

'You know... we've been through a lot. I really do think we were fated,' I said, gripping Clara's arm a little tighter.

'What is fated?' she replied. 'As far as I can tell, only two things are. Life... and death. All in between is a matter of happenchance. Luck. Essentially meaningless. What we live for... what we die for.'

The melancholy undertone of her words spoke volumes and I appreciated them for I had lived the same life as she. Still, I couldn't help but think we were looking over two different landscapes. I was seeing the literal, beautiful countryside that graced most of the view before our eyes, and she was seeing the desolate and alone, the black and the bleak of what lay beneath the caves. However, the direction of the conversation wasn't one I wished to continue.

After what seemed like a time much longer than it actually was, we concluded our sight seeing and descended back into the buildings. The silences continued to be awkward yet were broken up with small talk. Clara occasionally would ask if I was okay in my quiet and I was able to answer honestly that I was, while dishonestly concealing what was niggling at me.

As we approached the drop in the hill we were presented with two paths; one, the path we had walked up, which would lead us out right by the Percy Arms, and the other which would lead us into another part of the village which we had yet to explore. Not wanting to face the awkwardness of being sat only with Clara for a few hours in the wake of her revelation I gently directed us down the lesser travelled path, towards the unchartered territory.

After navigating the narrow bridge over the small stream which separated the homes from the hills, we immediately approached what appeared to be a small community centre although I couldn't tell on first impression if it was, or at least had been, a church. It was prefabricated and crude and rather unnecessary in its placement. As we walked closer to it my attention was drawn to the not exactly inconspicuous placard which declared 'PROPERTY AUCTION TODAY'. Our interest was instant; if only to see how it was done out of the city.

Once inside we were surprised to see that the spread of potential bidders was sparse; hardly the bubbling cauldron we had experienced on our sole occasion when we decided to take our baby steps into the business. I picked up a couple of the property brochures and handed one to Clara, flicking through one myself; the listings seemed more than just a little superfluous considering the numbers that had turned out and if I was being more than just a little honest, the appearance of those who were present did not strike me as people who would either harbour interest in purchasing the properties in the price ranges listed nor have the funds to do so.

That was, until, after flicking through the pages, I came across the listing for a 'Tŷ Glo'. I immediately felt as if there had been a mistake, some sort of printing error, for the house was listed at a mere £300. I read and read, looking for some kind of small print, but the words only served to further prick my intrigue and desire to discover more. Multiple bedrooms, bathrooms, owned by the locally renowned Roberts family for generations, partly restored but left unoccupied for years... There must be a catch, yet it seemed like a golden opportunity. As my eyes lifted up off of the page and glanced across to Clara's I could see she had seen the same and, more, appeared to feel the same. We both stuttered over words trying to make sense of the absurdity of it.

'Should...,' I tentatively began. 'Surely...'

'Well, what can... what shall we do?'

Neither of us appeared willing to commit on this outlandish idea without the other having spoken it. I gently placed my hands over Clara's and looked her in the eye.

'If you want it, we can get it.' 'But how... the house?'

Clara was concerned about the money we had lost. I had quickly calculated in my head that we had enough remaining capital to at least put an offer in — at this price — and then once we were able to juggle some funds around we would be able to decorate this vast home to our style and taste. As quickly as my mind had processed that buying the house could be something we could do, as soon as there was the merest of encouragement that Clara felt the same, I started to entertain the notion of this grand house, situated on its own small island, being one that she could not bear to not see filled with the activity of children. Not just one, but maybe two, three, four. Goodness, we could have a whole tribe. My thoughts all ran away from me as quickly as they came and I felt remarkably giddy.

'We can do it, if you want. We can,' I encouraged her.

Well, Clara went full steam ahead, so excited I could barely comprehend the words she was saying. The words 'castle' and 'hotel' were thrown around while she ran through lists of ideas she could do to an old Victorian home. 'I can't wait, I just can't wait', was a repeated mantra. I was so bemused by the speed of her conversation that I drifted away and was more gently comforted by the happiness in her voice.

My eyes took me around the room where I still felt oddly placed amongst the few people there, then they took me out of the window and back up the hills which we had just walked from. I arched my neck slightly to see more of the hill but I was pulled quickly by Clara which startled me — the auction of our dream house was about to begin.

'Next up... Lot 106... now let's see if we've got any interest in this one,' announced the auctioneer.

I had no idea of how long the auction had been running prior to our arrival but in the time we had been there it didn't seem as if there had been any interest in any of the other lots, the other houses. Maybe I hadn't noticed it because I was so consumed by the prospect of this house, or, maybe they too were all waiting to bid on our house.

'Tŷ Glo in nearby Dyffryn Du... Five bedrooms, two en suite... given a renovation and restoration by the Roberts family some years ago since when it has remained unoccupied. I'm sure we're all familiar with the property. For those who weren't, I'm sure you have familiarised yourself with it now from the notes in our prospectus.'

I was sure that in his last sentence, the auctioneer cocked

his head and looked suspiciously at Clara and I, as if we were naughty children for seemingly considering it. I looked around again — had this house at a bargain priced been promised to somebody else? Had one of these people in the auction room, as pleasant as they seemed but apparently without the means to buy such a piece of property, suffered the misfortune of losing this house and was here to watch it go for a relative pittance?

As a short silence fell over the room, the auctioneer coughed and composed himself.

'Right then. Tŷ Glo is listed at £300 — do I hear £300?'

Clara gripped my hand tightly. The first rule of an auction room, never go in on the first offer, evaluate your opposition.

'280?'

We glanced around the room. Surely. Surely. But no — no movement. I was tempted, at that moment, to raise my hand, and Clara could send that I was agitated, but held my hand as if to restrict it from moving for just a second.

'250?' invited the auctioneer, half-heartedly, before rapping almost instantly, 'I shall pass if there is no interest?'

Clara's hand shot up. The auctioneer gave a glare that said 'What on Earth are you doing?' and his eyes were so fixed on her that it caused every other pair of eyes in the room to move towards her too. Including mine! I wasn't sure if she had instantaneously become hideously disfigured such was the surprise everyone seemed to be looking at her with but no, she was confident and composed.

A few seconds passed and I wasn't sure if this was showmanship on Clara's part or if she was simply trying to confirm, but she said 'Here', leaving no doubt that she had placed a bid on the property and that this arm movement hadn't been some spasmodic impulse.

There was no competition — even at that price — and the auctioneer was so reluctant to bring his gavel down that for a fleeting second I thought he was waiting more for us to change our mind on the offer rather than waiting for someone to outbid us. Crazy!

We sorted out the paperwork rather swiftly — I was able to write a cheque for the amount and was confident that it would clear. There had been a moment where the auctioneer — Mr Roscoe, we learned his name was — thought he might have priced us out by adding the fee for the auction on top but the truth was even at £250, the house would have been an absolute bargain, and covering the cheque would have been no problem.

To be fair to the fellow, he was most helpful, explaining that the telephone line was disconnected at the house, but boasting that one of the many advantages of living in a small locality was that tradesmen were easily contactable. We were informed that they would send someone out to connect the line that evening.

We left, with assurance that the deeds and keys would be delivered to us at the Percy Arms, on our walk back to our hotel. We were so full of adrenalin that we could have walked back up the hill and around the long way but so full of excitement that our pressing need was to get back and celebrate.

If I am to be blunt and honest, any concerns of how inexpensive the house was had gone to the back of my mind. Clara and I had never ventured out of a London postcode area before...

well, there was the one time we went to Brighton for the day, but regardless, this was definitely the first and only time we had ventured north. It had been a source of great humour to us when we arrived into Wales as we joked we had finally visited another country. And now we had bought a house there, a very real commitment to living there or at least giving a significant proportion of our time up to travel and a temporary move. Could we make such a move? Would it put too much strain on our relationship? How would each of us individually cope with living in the relative wilderness, out of the City? I questioned myself on all of this but I knew it was futile because we had already made the decision. And that decision had been so *easy*. Those reservations were quelled by Clara's enthusiasm and neither of us could wait to celebrate.

Chapter Four
A Celebration

WHEN WE arrived back at the Percy Arms at around 4pm I am glad to say that it was the hub of activity I had pictured in my imagination the previous night; there were drinkers out on the benches all enjoying a rapturous joke in spite of the cold, no doubt warmed by the jugs of alcohol they were consuming or had already consumed.

Once we got inside the warmth of the pub hit us so strongly that we immediately sought to take our coats off and make ourselves comfortable at the nearest available table.

'Here they are!' Hector proclaimed in his most friendly voice. 'And what have you two lovebirds been doing? Enjoying the fair sights of our beautiful county no doubt? Can I get you a drink?'

We had already become used to his multiple questions, and realised that the last one was more of a statement than a question.

'Well, actually...' I started.

'Ooh, that sounds ominous. You haven't got yourselves into any trouble have you now?'

'No, not at all, nothing like that...'

'We bought a house!' Clara couldn't help but interrupt with her squeal.

'Ah well... in that case... it's a celebration!' insisted Hector. He retreated to the bar and after what seemed like a considerable effort against his own gait he was able to wrench a dusted bottle of champagne from a high shelf.

'I'm a welcoming gentleman you know, but not all is free...' he said, waving the bottle.

'That's fine,' I insisted, boldly. 'And why don't you join us?'

So Hector and Lillian came and sat with us as we told them of our day, how we'd enjoyed seeing the village and our views up the hills, and we discussed something of the old, disused mines.

'I'm as proud as anyone of this little place but come now, I can't as see why that's cause for actually buying a house here... living here?' asked Hector.

'Well, if I may...' I began, breaking off only to pop the bottle open at what I felt was a subtle hint by my host (to the obvious and inevitable cheers and 'hurray' as the champagne began to bubble). 'Yes... well... Clara and I almost fell upon this little auction room... at the prefab by the stream'.

'Ah you mean Roscoe's.'

'Yes, yes that's the place... well... anyway, we were looking through the properties and couldn't believe how inexpensive everything was. It really is quite incredible.'

'Lot more land up here lad. Not quite as packed in like sardines as you are down there.'

'Yes, quite... we really couldn't resist.'

'So then we'll be neighbours? Tell me you bought the farm, old Snowdon's farm? I'll be glad to see the back o' that old coot.'

'No, not exactly,' interjected Clara. 'The house is in Dyffryn Du, it's called Ty Glo... it has its own land and everything.'

Hector's eyes sharpened. 'Tŷ Glo, you say...' he trailed off, though I expected him to continue. He did after a few moments. 'How much do you know?'

'Know of what?' I asked.

'The house, the area.'

'We know it hasn't been occupied for some time... but it has been renovated fairly recently by the Roberts family?'

'Yes... well, the Roberts family,' Hector started and shifted himself as if he was to tell an epic story. 'Elfyn Roberts was a fine man. He made his fortune in farming and then land, you know. I should know, bought this pub from him, and he drove a hard price. But he was a good man. At one point I reckoned he owned around three quarters of Dyffryn Du. Maybe even more.'

'Did he live in Tŷ Glo?' I interrupted. I was glad to hear of the history of the area but rather impatient as to the point of where it was leading.

Hector looked at me as if I was out of my mind to have asked.

'No, no, he didn't live there.'

'Pardon, it's just that you know... you speak of Mr Roberts... Elfyn Roberts... as if he were Lord of the Manor and so I just assumed that the house seems fit for someone of that stature.'

'Oh it's fit for something alright... I see where you're coming from. I know what you mean. But no he didn't live there. He did live in a house just as majestic. But there was a warmth to the Roberts'. No, he bought Tŷ Glo to save that community.'

'Save them from what?' Silence.

'Save them from what?' I repeated.

'They say the house and the land is haunted.'

Clara and I couldn't help but burst out laughing.

'What nonsense!' Clara said. 'Wonderful nonsense though. That would make an excellent selling point for... God, I don't know. We could make it a hotel. Convert it in to a bed and breakfast. Come and stay at the haunted house!'

After composing myself and listening to Clara, I noticed Hector's expression hadn't changed from the serious one he had delivered his previous statement with.

'When you say haunted, what do you mean?'

'Well, you hear stories of what happened up there... but we're talking fifty or sixty years ago and even longer. You're probably right, old wives tales. I respected Elfyn and that's why I can't bring myself to joke about it.'

'Of course... I... we meant no malice. He must have been quite rich if he was able to make such a purchase and not even have the cause to live there.'

'Oh he was, but not frivolous.'

'So why are they selling the house?'

'Elfyn died around forty years ago, only a year or so after I bought from him. His wife died around eight or nine years after and they had no children so all the property and everything he owned... well, there was no-one to claim it, until someone came forward saying he was a nephew on the wife's side. He had the paperwork and everything. So... he was from Leeds, or somewhere, not from around here. He had no connection to the community. A lot of people lost their homes. He was only after some money, quick money. He moved up here... James, I think his name was. James Appleton.'

'And this James...'

'Oh, I don't know him. Can't says as I've ever met him. But you hear things. And I've never heard good things. He's sold off most of the property and land. A lot of people were forced out, people who were tenants couldn't afford the rent. He put it up because they refused to buy outright. Because of its... and because of his reputation he's struggled to sell Tŷ Glo.'

'Yes, we were taken aback by how inexpensive it was.'

'That don't surprise me,' he continued. 'I'm not trying to scare you. I only just met you, I like the look of you. People in this community, even ours, are loathe to give more money to him. They talk about the ghosts... look, as far as I know, nothing's ever happened up there. Not in my lifetime. There was some damage in the war but we were all affected by that. There's an appearance to the old place. It's hard to get to by itself, eh, there's nothing around it for some distance. There were a few houses and a church the locals used but they've all been knocked down. They went before the First World War so the house is by itself and stands out like a sore thumb. My only hope is that you didn't pay a lot of money for it, I would hate to think he's continued to benefit.'

'Not at all... my hand was almost trembling as I wrote the cheque, I thought it was a mistake!'

'So it's all done then? You Southern lot don't hang around...'

'I promise you we have no bad intentions. It was purely opportunistic... chance...,' I realised I was repeating myself, and to an extent, I felt as if I was still trying to convince myself it had actually happened.

'So, what do you plan to do with it then?' enquired Lillian. It was enough of a question to set us off on a more lighthearted track of conversation, with Clara explaining her ideas. Privately I was slightly disappointed by the numerous references to the house being developed into a hotel of some sort but I still remained hopeful that in any event, once we saw the house and land, it may alter her plans for the future.

As we retreated to our room before our evening meal, slightly light-headed from the bubbles we had taken on an empty stomach, Clara and I discussed the practicalities of how we would move forward. It was far from an ideal situation we had placed ourselves in but now we had taken such an uncharacteristic gamble we had to deal with the consequences and we realised that logically it meant we may need to spend some time apart in order to sort out our affairs in London and ensure no time was wasted on our new home. There was some deliberation and contention; we both agreed that it was more sensible if I stayed in order to do any of the 'handyman' work that was required at the house — and it was better if Clara sorted all the paperwork out back home because she was used to dealing with that side of the business. Still, I didn't feel comfortable that Clara would be driving by herself and we discussed it over a couple of hours. Being as persistent and strong as she is, she was able to convince me that she would be fine driving back up from London.

Clearly, then, my plans for a romantic getaway had been put on hold, but I hoped that they had accelerated to a place I'd never dreamed and that our new abode and excitement would lead to a fairytale, happy ending. The following morning I saw Clara off at Aberaernavon Station, sorry for the length of the journey she was to face and worried that she may get lost during one of the changes. By the end of all of my fussing I'm sure she was growing frustrated and was quite glad to be on the train. She was full of smiles as she boarded, giving me a warm hug and a tender kiss, telling me she would see me in two days. 'At our new home', she beamed.

Chapter Five
Home

I WAS able to put aside my nervousness concerning Clara's trip home, and rather easily, I am a little ashamed to admit. She would have understood and surely have been in the same position as I was.

For it wasn't every day that we were going to benefit from the sort of fortune we'd enjoyed the previous day. In fact I dare say if we had swapped positions, then Clara would be far more excited than I was, to see the house, to begin to visualise how all those dreams she had had from the few pictures she had seen might become reality. I also knew that it was undoubtedly better that I was the one to see the actual reality first, if one of us had to. Both of us had grown so disappointed and underwhelmed by our experiences in London that I couldn't bear for this excitement to wind up as an anti-climax.

I took a taxi back to the Percy Arms where we had arranged for the keys and relevant documents pertaining to the house to be delivered. Hector had offered to drive me there — a generous gesture as the drive was at least forty minutes. Having asked us of our plans early that morning, he insisted he help and also said he would keep a room available for us if needed. If I am as astute a judge of character as I like to think I am, I would also hazard a reasonable guess that Hector had grown curious of the legend of this 'Tŷ Glo', after he confessed he not only had never been there, but had only visited Dyffryn Du in his younger days, and certainly not since James Appleton had become something of a property king. He — Hector — didn't strike me as the kind that scared easily but I had also felt his respect for Mr Elfyn Roberts to be so true and deeply felt that he wanted to go and see for himself. Additionally, he may well have been offended by the flippant and jovial way Clara and I initially took his comments, and was determined to show he wasn't afraid.

Once back at the Percy Arms, Hector was as bold and brash as expected, welcoming me back as he stood by his motor, indicating that he wanted to get a move on right away, which suited me just fine.

Our journey was ostensibly most pleasant. We drove through a couple of small villages, the names of which I didn't remember although Hector was keen to tell me lots of facts about. The conversation filled the time and filled the silence that I was internally occupying with thoughts of Clara's own journey home. I felt that — I knew that — she'd be fine. I had been re-assured by her comments that she still loved me but now, having time to settle by myself after the events of the last day or so, the weight of what she had said about not having children did begin to settle on me. How true was it, how sincere had she been? Was it a spur of the moment thing, or was this something that had always been there that I had somehow never picked up on? A part of me had come away from that brief interchange wondering if she even realised how much the words had affected me and even though I should have felt re-assured, I was now wondering if our move to Tŷ Glo was going to represent some-thing of a make or break point in our marriage.

I was certain that financially it was a very smart move for us to make — how could it not be? I had reasoned with myself that with rising property prices we could simply do nothing and probably double our money, or more than, within a few years. I also knew from experience that a financial profit alone wouldn't be enough to give Clara the satisfaction she sought. I didn't know what would be, though. How could I have gone from feeling I knew everything about my wife, this person I'd spent so much of my life with, to now feeling like there was so much I didn't know of her?

'Here it is,' announced Hector, interrupting my train of thought. 'Dyffryn Du.'

The unspectacular, unassuming village before my eyes was hardly worthy of such a grand introduction. Just like the oth-ers, really, with its winding, uncompromising roads, and small cobbled houses which seemed squeezed in to the small hills on which they sat, side by side. As we drove through I noticed how empty it was; nobody on the streets, nobody on the greenery or parks, nobody around their houses. Only when we got to the church and there appeared to be plenty of people on the grounds did I realise that it was a Sunday, and so I was re-assured by the evident sense of community which I had felt was preva-lent in Aberaernavon. It also went some way to comforting me as I had half expected to arrive in a village where everybody hated one another, or kept to themselves, going by Hector's words about the place. I felt comfortable enough to raise the topic.

'I must say, from your warning, I had prepared myself for

some sort of anti-social atmosphere but it does appear anything but,' I said.

'Yes, they're all Appleton's, give or take. A few of his friends. I think a few stayed on, managed to keep their houses,' Hector replied.

As we left the village our ascent up a hill meant it was almost instantly beneath us and within but a few moments I was able to gaze backwards and see it all within one panoramic view. Against my vivid memory of yellow lights and tall houses, the vast size of the City I'd grown up in, I found myself fascinated by the concept that all of the various stages of life, all that some people had ever known, was being played out in a valley which was all contained in one vision. It was remarkable and liberating, although I could almost hear Clara's own rebuttal as if she were sat right next to me, arguing that it would be most suffocating. As usual, she would have more than a salient point.

The countryside was seemingly full of surprises and Hector probably must have thought me a naive child, full of wonderment, by the expression on my face with every new turn of the corner. As I finally moved my head forwards to the views in front, though, I was genuinely astounded to see a veritable transformation. From the small inclines and gentle hills we have travelled through, now we were presented with a perfectly flat and level landscape. A thin fog, a cloud, almost luminous in colour, provided a blanket over our view which made it difficult to see more than roughly one hundred feet in front. Hector was quiet, happy to drive, and the silence added to the serene atmosphere.

The November sun had begun its descent and its obscured faltering of light gave a somewhat dull feel to the view but I attributed that down to the mist as much as anything. It was easy to understand that on a clearer day, like yesterday, the scenery would have been much more beautiful than the word could truly give justice.

'This is the start of your land,' Hector informed me, much to my surprise.

'How you can tell,' he continued, 'is the start of the hill.'

'Yes,' I said, weakly offering something to the conversation. Hector was right, of course — the rough track had now become a makeshift road that was snaking its way up a rather steep climb. The 'road', if it were to be described as such, was quite narrow — I had found roads in the north to be far narrower than they were back home and this pathway was narrower still, occasionally looking like it may draw so thin that Hector's motor may have trouble maintaining its course. From the passenger side, I looked down, noting how harsh the incline had become. As we continued to travel, I noticed a stream running down the valley which had opened out in front of us into a sizable lake. For each passing moment I found myself fixated in the small pockets of scenery I was able to see, mesmerised by all which was now ours, and giddy with excitement about what I might see once the sky was clear.

All of a sudden, sure enough, around two hundred feet in front of us, revealed by the dissipation of the clouds, Tŷ Glo appeared. It was quite magnificent. Breathtaking. The view of the house was unobstructed; the pictures in the brochures appeared to show some greenery and birch trees in front but all were gone to present the most picturesque front view of a building that I had ever seen. Even Hector was silent — and though we had not spoken for a few minutes as we scaled the hill, I couldn't help but think that he too had been stunned by just how beautiful this marvelous construction was to the eye.

'Imagine the stories it could tell if it could speak,' I pondered aloud.

'Will you be okay here, by yourself?' asked Hector.

'Yes, I imagine I shall be fine.'

'Have you enough provisions?'

'Lillian gave us plenty, I'm sure she gave enough to keep me fed for a week, and Clara will be up soon.'

'At least let us see if there is a way you can contact us, a working telephone at least.'

'Honestly, we should be fine, I should be fine.'

'See that back there, it's called The Snake.'

'It does seem rather narrow but as I am on foot I...'

'It doesn't matter whether on foot or on wheel. You'll walk among the clouds up here and they come in. We get a lot of rain. So the rain comes in and you won't be able to see in front of you. Gets too dark and there's nothing to stop you falling over the side. It would not be wise to try. So I'm going to need to know if I can contact you.'

I was so eager to explore the house and its surroundings that I was almost reluctant to accede to Hector's request but I did so in the knowledge that I may well require assistance should I encounter any unforeseen problems and, to be honest, I had grown surprisingly fond and comfortable in Hector's company in the little over 36 hours I had known him. I was also most grateful for his knowledge of the area because without it I would undoubtedly have found myself worried.

Hector and I got out of the car and walked towards the house — my initial thought was that less than an hour before, I had been able to capture an entire village in my line of vision, and here I was stood in front of a house — a considerable distance away — and it filled my panoramic view from left to right. I could feel a power emanating from it, a strength of character unlike anything I had ever experienced from bricks and mortar.

The deforestation looked fairly recent, with tree stumps looking peached and fresh rather than deadened. It accentuated the isolation of the property and made me wonder just how strong it might look on a clearer day with nothing obscuring its majesty.

It's no exaggeration to say I had already felt quite a strong connection with Tŷ Glo and was overcome with the thrill of owning it. I could barely wait for Clara to come and see it for herself, my only hope was that she would be treated to a clearer day than I had been.

We approached the front of the house and I unlocked the door, revealing inside a marvellous grand hallway with a large, bold staircase. What hit me first, though, was an overwhelming familiarity. As accustomed and used as I had been to what I felt was a very comfortable three bedroom house in London, I couldn't help but romanticize about potentially settling down in such a home. It was a feeling which grew with each step I took and each thing I discovered about this grand old place.

First things first, I thought. I couldn't give myself to adventure until I had dealt with the practicalities and so I searched for a telephone — the library was the first room I entered and there was one on the desk. It was oak paneled and regal, more like a room I would expect to encounter in a solicitor's office from my experience than one I could ever have expected to use for my personal leisure.

'Here,' I told Hector. 'I'll just see if it works.'

I picked up the telephone and sure enough, there was a dialling tone.

'It works.'

'I'll have to leave you the number of the pub... I haven't got a pen. Or paper come to that,' said Hector, fumbling in his pockets.

'No need to worry — I still have it from our booking,' I reassured him.

'Of course, of course... well... I can't leave without knowing your power is on.'

He tried a light and it came on without a problem at all. He then walked back into the hallway and tried the light, where it once again came on instantaneously.

'There... seems like they have set you up good to go.'

'It did say there had been restoration. To be honest we weren't sure what that meant.'

As far as I could tell, the house appeared as if it hadn't been lived in for the period of time it had been owned by the Roberts'. Perhaps even longer, I couldn't tell. And yet the effort to clean it by this James Appleton, or whoever he had employed, meant there was no dust, and everything seemed just as it might, albeit frozen in time. To that end, the home held considerable charm. I had gathered some experience in interior design but not enough to give me a discernible eye.

'If there has been any, I wouldn't be able to tell you. How much did you say you paid for this place?'

'I'm afraid that matters of finance are matters I like to keep private... I'm sure you appreciate,' I said. I felt slightly reluctant as I was certain Hector's question was out of curiosity rather than anything sinister or laced with any sort of ulterior motive.

'Suit yourself... But I saw it listed for under £500, and you surely will have paid even less. I've never seen this place from the inside before, but now I have, I wonder what they were thinking...'

'I'm as surprised as you.'

'Maybe... maybe we were just all put off by the story. Nobody gave it due consideration... If I could rewind the clock a few hours, knowing what I know, I would have no problem buying this place for that price.'

'Sorry Hector, but I'm not considering offers,' I laughed.

'So long as we're invited for the dinner parties,' joked Hector. 'Seems you got all in place here. I'll be on my way. Now it will be five in the afternoon before I'll be able to get back over. So if you need anything you'll have to wait until then.'

'Honestly, I appreciate that. But I should be fine. It's not long after two and I seem to have enough. But of course if I need anything you'll be my first call, now I know I can.'

'Well,' said Hector, turning to leave. 'Don't be afraid to. Call, that is.'

With that, he gave a tip of his hat and saw himself out. I remained in the library, still astounded by the size and quality of the craftmanship in the oak cabinets and furniture. It was only after the sound of Hector's motor spluttering and stirring into life, and then gradually fading into the distance, that I began to realise just how silent the house was.

I liked it.

CHAPTER SIX
The Explorer

ONCE I had ventured into the downstairs rooms — the lounge, a sitting room, a library, the vast kitchen and the pantry — I decided to go upstairs and see what of the view I could make out from the windows. As I ascended the staircase I felt like a young child at Christmas, rather evocative as I remembered my own childhood, racing down stairs just like these, rather than up. Of course, racing up a solid wood staircase consumes much more energy than going down, but I was still eager and not drained by the time I had reached the top. My plan had been to race to the first open door but to my surprise all were shut; I then decided to go to the first room which overlooked the hill, 'The Snake', to see if I could make out Hector from the height.

The door was jammed, initially, but after I gave it some force and seemingly failed to open it, I gave it the slightest of nudges and it opened easily. I was surprised by what I saw, not for the first time — a grand four poster bed, a cabinet and wardrobe, all matching and immaculately crafted. Surely not every room was furnished to such a high standard? I felt as if there was some small print I had missed in the contract and decided to myself that I would go over it later. I also made the decision to not grow too attached to the furnishings just incase someone would come to take them away. The grandness of the room had momentarily taken my breath away but I strode to the window to look over the valley — some of the fog had cleared, but in any event, where I imagined Hector must have been was too far out of sight to have seen him even on a clear day, now. I was able to see for what seemed like at least a mile in front of the house, though the descent of the hill began around two hundred yards from our new home. Even though much of the land appeared to be wasteland, there was a beauty in the openness, the space and the untouched, natural element of it all. I could notice that to my left, I could now see the mines I had seen with Clara, in the far away distance, on the other side of the lake.

Shapes to the right caught my eye; what appeared to be a graveyard, or burial plot, with a few scattered headstones that were neither properly organised nor kept well. It stood to reason that on land that had been the exclusive ownership of only one or two families over the last fifty years, they would have their burial plots here. I was curious to learn more about that and the history of the house that we had adopted.

I walked out of the bedroom and towards one of the rooms that would overlook the back of the house. My initial eagerness to see things that had grabbed my imagination prior to entering the house was now giving way to the curiosity of the objects within it. I expected, of course, a certain level of class, but I had not expected it to be furnished the way it had been, right down to the pictures which hung on the wall. There were wonderfully painted pictures of scenery not too dissimilar to that which we had driven through in Dyffryn Du, and it emphasised the local pride. It made me feel as if the house had a really important standing in the community, a noble and respected residence for those who had once lived here. This old place was already feeling like home. I was already feeling like I belonged.

I passed a couple of these pictures, stopping to acknowledge and appreciate them on the way to the back bedrooms. It took passing them to even notice them, though, as their darkness blended in perfectly with the dark patterned wallpaper. The house appeared as if it were at least two hundred years old and the decor was dated but as far as I could tell it still looked as if it had most recently been decorated around twenty years ago. The upstairs corridor squared itself around the top of the hallway, making the below resemble an atrium, and the lack of natural lighting made some features of the upper floor almost indistinguishable. A complete contrast to the striking personality of the house itself.

The first door I approached was considerably easier to open, as straightforward as any other. This room was not quite as large or proud as the other but still a guest room which was twice the size of our master bedroom back in London. It was funny, but such were my growing expectations of the house, part of me expected it to be even bigger and more luxurious than the first bedroom. I walked straight for the window and any temporary disappointment I had allowed myself to feel was replaced by the amazement of the most wonderful of views behind the house.

There was a small shed, or outhouse, around twenty yards from the back of the house, and around two hundreds yards away to the far left — now visible, as the clouds were clearing

— I could make out what appeared to the fragmented stone remains of another small building. I was no expert in historical rural architecture but the assembly of stone and the remaining structure of an arch suggested it might well once have been a chapel or even a small church. Obscured behind the arch were a few more gravestones. I could see the remains of maybe four or five other houses, the boundaries determined by walls no taller than a foot with bricks discarded in the proximity.

For some reason, looking out of the back of the house gave me a cold feeling. Where the front had been welcoming, regal and sturdy, the back appeared hostile, secretive and bleak. For what reason, I am unable to describe, because to the naked eye there was no difference. Perhaps, I felt, it may have been the remnants of the fog casting an unfavourable atmosphere. Beyond the gravestones I could make out the water's edge and something of a shore. There was a very special beauty unique to Tŷ Glo, quite unlike anything I'd ever experienced. I'd spent little over half an hour in this house and yet the emotions I had felt made me think of Clara and how she must have felt when spending time in the first apartment we bought in Westminster. From what I could see, Clara wouldn't need to do much work at all, although knowing her like I did, she would probably seek to turn the whole place upside down. What did I know, after all!

I considered the way I had instantly felt about the back of the house and decided to go out and properly explore it, and get the chance to feel the air on my skin. I walked down the stairs and out of the front door, deciding to walk to the right and past the gravestones I had seen at the front. I wondered if they might continue all the way around to the chapel.

It was cold when Hector had driven me to the house but it

had turned bitter and fierce as I walked outdoors, as if there was something in the atmosphere resisting the imminent onset of dark. I walked closer to the gravestones and I could not make out the names or dates because of the lichen and fungi that dominated most of them. It appeared as if the grounds had been dug up and tampered with which caused me to feel a great sadness.

I remembered the caretaker of the graveyard where my parents are buried once scolding me after finding me attempting to clean their gravestones. We had spent so long choosing the most beautiful marble stone for my mother and for the first year after she passed we visited every few weeks. Life goes on, and those visits were reduced to every year. On the third year I noticed the stone had become rather dirty so returned the following week with a desire to clean the stone. I had been scrubbing away for a good fifteen minutes when the caretaker came up and stopped me. He insisted that in applying so much pressure, I was causing more damage, and doing the stone more harm than good in the long term, ruining the surface and therefore destroying the point of choosing marble in the first place.

Still, there was an over-zealous approach to cleanliness and presentation and then the other end of the spectrum, leaving a stone completely unkept and giving it no attention whatsoever. It was a shame but a natural consequence of having loved ones buried on private land; once the family moves away, there is no particular obligation for the new family or new tenants to give due care and attention. It made me contemplate the loneliness and obscurity the previous owners of the house must have felt. My own imagery — and indeed, the immediate reaction of Hector — had been the social potential of such a venue, and it seemed such a waste and a shame that it appeared not only to have not been used as such, but also, absolutely neglected. Surely the location of the house hadn't been enough on its own to have deterred visitors?

I found myself dwelling and decided to pull myself away and continue to explore the outside and so walked down the left hand side of the house. I was surprised that in actual fact it was just simple greenery, with no more gravestones until the back of the chapel. Of course, the stonework there had been arranged particularly for its more traditional setting in a former life but it still felt eerie, as if created for this moment, to scare somebody out of their wits in our modern age. I was too wise — or, that should be, too old — to be frightened by a masonry settlement. Surely. Sometimes, rational thought goes out of the window when confronted with something that we have been so indoctrinated to accept as a moment that should be terrifying. In the moments before I approached what seemed like it would have been the entrance, although precious little remained of anything to suggest it might have been, my body provided a strong hesitance against my own will, as if to suggest it was a bad idea.

Poppycock, I told myself. I remembered how Clara and I had laughed at the notion, the suggestion that our new home had unwelcome guests from another world and I allowed myself a chuckle at how bizarre I had allowed the solitude and quiet to affect me. Quite foolish. I walked through the 'altar', and noticed the rows which once must have provided seating had all but eroded. The character of the land was compelling. Was this small area once the central hub of the immediately local community?

I ventured as far as the gravestones but was disappointed to find they were in the same state of disrepair as the others. The house, the land, remained almost a complete mystery. It wasn't too far to reach the unsteady ground which eventually went from puddles and the boggy underfoot to completely submerged. Some of the gravestones had fallen victim to the growing stream and I wondered if perhaps it was the changing stability or increasing volume of the wetlands around the stream which had devalued the land and property. I could already see that it was impossible to farm or grow any meaningful produce. Perhaps there were concerns about the management of the water and the damage it may cause to the property. If horticulture was unreasonable then even simple gardening seemed pointless. An interest for the sake of having one in all of this isolation? Tŷ Glo exuded such a strong personality that any decoration may have detracted from the grand vision. It couldn't have added anything to it. It required no extra vanity.

I wandered over to the outhouse and was quite delighted to see it was empty. What it once housed I could only guess, but it must have been gutted in preparation for the sale. It would make an excellent retreat for me, a workshop where I could create and invent to my heart's content without dirtying any of the dignified innards of the house. Yes, I could already envision many fruitful hours here. I checked in my pockets for the key so I might have a look on the inside of the small building but, alas, they weren't on the ring — they must be in the house somewhere.

I strolled around the other side of the house to the front and wondered how long I must have been outside, because the sun had set and the dark was fast approaching. The outhouse had really captured my imagination and so I felt encouraged to go inside and perhaps see if there was anything I could do immediately, admittedly armed with only a toolbox I had borrowed from Hector. Whatever — I had to do something to wile away the hours until 10 o'clock, as I knew that Clara would be home by then, and I knew she would be waiting for me to call.

I decided I would begin 'work' in the second bedroom. I thought long and hard and settled with the opinion that I would prefer Clara to see the house in much the same state I had on my first viewing; simultaneously, I acknowledged that she would not be at all happy if she were to imagine I had done nothing but joyously romp around the property with glee and delight. It was a tough decision because I could almost hear Clara tutting that I had tampered with the original condition I had discovered the house in but I concluded that she would forgive me in the circumstances for choosing the second bedroom I had gone into.

It was still easier said than done. I opened the door full of anticipation and with a smile on my face but upon looking around I struggled to find anything I should start with. After thinking for quite some time — I should imagine I spent at least twenty minutes, just stood, deliberating — I noticed that one of the floorboards appeared to be slightly rotting, or deteriorated, in the corner. At last! An imperfection, however minor, something I could attempt to fix. I carefully dislodged and removed the faulty board, anxiously taking my time so as not to cause any further damage. Once it was lifted, I was able to remove the surrounding boards from underneath, safe in the knowledge they could easily be put back without anyone ever having known they had been moved. I was also pleased to find that upon closer inspection, the floorboards were elm, fitting for an house of this age. It should be straightforward to replace or mend the piece of wood, though not quite so to try and replicate the same kind of wear in the finish to ensure it didn't look out of place.

The frames supporting the floor were quite magnificent, I imagined that they were just as sturdy as the day they were put in place, a testament to the wonderful workmanship I so appreciated and also the care with which the house had been looked after in. I ducked my head in between the frames and gave them a knock to confirm their strength. Something caught my eye amid the dust, something glistening in the small pockets of light. I tried to reach it but was unable — it was just out of arms reach. It was futile to exert myself; I knew I couldn't contort my arm or hand to the length required, so pulled myself back out of the hole. I thought for a moment whether I ought to pull yet another two boards up in order to provide a far simpler access but decided at that point I may as well, as it wouldn't provide any noticeable detriment to the flooring if I was careful with my replacement.

I did so with the utmost of delicacy and attention, still with the approach that I was handling someone else's property rather than my own. When I finally reached my treasure I was bemused — it was a silver metal box, approximately the same size of a shoe box. It was rather unlike anything I'd ever seen before and so its contents were equally mysterious. And still it, much like the house, seemed familiar. The sense of reward I felt upon getting my hands on it was as if I had re-discovered a childhood toy. Immediately my concentration had drifted — I observed the now untidy room and laughed at the boyish way in which I appeared to have been captivated by all that was new. At the same time, that thought made me realise that I had been quite indulgent all afternoon. I placed the box on the bed and worked with a renewed discipline to replace all of the floorboards, as meticulously as I had taken them up. I admit that I was rather proud with the ease at which I was able to put them all back. A little too proud in fact — for a second I felt a great satisfaction, as if I were the one who had put it together in the first place some two hundred or so years earlier. Foolish, really.

I went downstairs and had a look through the provisions which Lillian had sent with me. There were tins but also a couple of sandwiches — ham — which I was relieved and grateful for because I had grown rather tired after my various exploits through the day. So tired, in fact, that I glanced at my watch in the hope that time had somehow accelerated to 9:50pm or a time in the vicinity, so that I might just have time to eat my sandwich and then ring Clara on the telephone. It was only 8:12pm. Lillian had also kindly packed in a small bottle of brandy which was welcome indeed. I don't suppose a small glass of brandy and a ham sandwich was a conventional dinner to mark the first evening in my new home but I had grown too fatigued to really care. And, honestly, I quite enjoyed my makeshift meal. The sandwich was filling — the bread tasted as if it had been homemade, which wouldn't have surprised me — and the brandy provided much warmth against the growing cold. Despite my best efforts to prolong my eating for as long as possible, my hunger got the better of me and the sandwich was devoured in a short time. I contemplated making more food but couldn't muster the energy... I pondered even having a bath to eat up more minutes but knew that the second I relaxed in warm water, my eyes would drop and I would give in to sleep.

I took an extra brandy through to the library — I thought that maybe, reading a book may keep my mind occupied, and in any event, I considered the library to be far more comfortable than the lounge. The lounge was an area I felt ought to be occupied by a larger number, company, to regale in conversation. There was no shame in enjoying your own company with a good book. The convenience of the telephone was just an added bonus.

A quite marvellous feature of the library was the huge coal fire and although I had seen it earlier, it was only on truly embracing the cold that I observed the true functionality. It was a centrepiece worthy of it's eponymity. It would have looked wonderfully majestic when used for purpose and, with the proximity to the mines, at some point, coal would have been in plentiful supply. I considered the lunacy which must have possessed whoever decided to remove all the trees, precious fuel, and I couldn't fathom it. It couldn't be helped. I realized that the outhouse must have been used to store coal.

I perused the selection of books and saw a number of atlases and maps; world and local history references. Of those that involved fiction, well, they must have belonged to a woman, as there appeared to be a great number of romance novels. The kind I would normally consider to be a little trashy, the property of the sort of individual seeking thrills in an otherwise dull life. I found that thought rather ironic — this houses, of all places, lended itself to all kinds of romantic thoughts. Even now, as it was. I could only imagine how it may once have looked at its proudest.

Giving way to frivolous temptation I decided to read one of these novels and looked for the most clichéd name I could set my eyes upon. 'A Lover's Revenge', I decided upon, and I rather enjoyed the introduction, setting the scene of a woman who discovered her lover was married by complete accident. It was my tiredness rather than my unexpected enjoyment of the story which ruined my concentration and made me constantly gaze at my watch, willing the second hand to jolly the minute hand into a swifter action. I gave up on the book and when the clock struck nine I decided I could wait no longer, and went to the desk to call Clara.

Fortunately, she was home. She seemed more excited to talk to me than I her, which was very welcome indeed, as she fired questions at me about the house. Was it as big as I thought? How vast was the land? How big were the rooms? How was the view? What had I done? I attempted to answer her with matched enthusiasm but she could tell by the slowness of my voice that I was quite tired. She was sympathetic, urging me to go and get some sleep, though keen to add, 'You'll need energy for all the work you'll be doing tomorrow!'

I barely got to ask her about her own day but she knew that wasn't out of selfishness. After all, Clara had dominated the conversation, and it was more than evident in her voice that she had arrived home without any concern. She would not have concealed it if it had been otherwise. It was strange, but the longer the call went on, the more awake I felt, and the less keen I was to leave the telephone. Of course, I missed Clara terribly even though it had been just a few hours, but it was more than that, it was the basic human resistance to being alone. It may have been nothing more than the lowering temperatures reminding me all too well of the isolation but as we reached the natural conclusion of our discussion I was absolutely reluctant to hang up.

'Darling, you really should get some sleep,' Clara said.

'It's funny, but I feel more awake now. Honestly, I could talk for a while longer,' I insisted.

'Well... I've had a long day myself, remember,' she reminded me. 'I could do with going to bed.'

With that, we told each other 'I love you' and said farewell. It was with a heavy heart that I placed the telephone on its receiver and I kept hold of it for a moment, wondering whether I might call Hector. I could call with the excuse that I needed fuel for the fire. No — I straightened myself. I had not wanted Clara to know I felt a little uneasy and I certainly didn't want to give that impression to anyone else. Besides, I would have to get up early. I didn't want to bother Hector with a journey all the way out to pick me up and then drop me off again early. Even if I called him to bring out some wood, then I should have to wait for that time, and then test the fire — probably in front of him to justify his journey and give him warmth that he would undoubtedly require — and I was already tired as it was. Even after all of that, I would still be on my own, and it would be much later. Clara was right, I was just too tired, over-thinking and over complicating matters. I pushed myself out of the chair at the desk where I had become a little too comfortable, and left the library, turning off the light.

As I entered the hallway, I felt the bitter cold as if someone had left the door open all evening, and so opted to go and take another quick drink of brandy to warm myself up. I was tempted to take the rest of the bottle with me to bed and continue to read the book I had started but decided against it, reasoning that the sooner I went to sleep, the better.

The bathroom was so cold that I decided that dental hygiene could wait until the morning, and instead went to the master bedroom, and made straight for the bed. I pulled back the protective sheet and was pleasantly surprised to find it immaculately presented, with clean satin sheets covered by a large throw. The throw itself appeared to be quite dusty so I picked it up and attempted to beat it against the wall — it caused me to cough and splutter quite violently so I didn't care to repeat it. I knew, however, that with the cold as it was, it wouldn't be wise to sleep without it, so put it back on the bed and thought to myself that I would properly beat or clean the throw the next day. It looked more than adequate for a night's sleep. I should sleep quite soundly. I sat on the side of the bed, and knocked back my last drink of brandy, before wrapping myself warm in the blankets and pulling the throw up to my midriff. Heaven.

I was quite at ease, permitting the natural flow of the unconscious to come and take me, yet as strange as it sounds, the complete and utter silence disturbed me. In London, I had been used to sleeping against a backdrop of traffic. It was never quieter than a gentle hum of motors intermittently driving up and down the high street at night. Here in the hills, there was nothing, and I would even have welcomed the sound of the wind to have caused a rustle in the branches of the few remaining overgrown bushes and sparse trees shed of their leaves outside. But there was nothing.

And it was unsettling.

Again, I felt myself growing more awake, and debated with myself whether I ought to go back downstairs and call Hector after all. All in all, I felt foolish. I forced my thoughts back to

Clara and her excited patter on the telephone earlier. My, I couldn't wait for her to see the house. I couldn't wait to see what she would do. I had gone around it and felt that my own footsteps were causing a blemish but she would know just what to do to make it even better, even grander.

Because of the strange mood I found myself in, it wasn't long before those procrastinations once more featured negative events. Being alone out here, not being able to talk to another, made me wonder if everything I was thinking was completely irrational. I had heard of cabin fever but thought that was something that only occurred after days and days of isolation in the wilderness. I was quite close to 'civilisation' and at any rate had only been by myself for a few hours yet I couldn't pacify myself with what I considered to be a logical explanation.

I once more thought about the house and what it represented, about Clara's words about not wanting children. The longer I spent here and thought about how nice it would be if there were a veritable bunch of hyperactive sprogs running around the place and getting underneath our feet, the more I realised that it had nothing to do with location, and more, my desire for children was really rather great. Clara had been honest with me but had I been honest with her, or even myself?

That was a conversation to have with her on another day and I was determined not to go to bed on a sour note, especially after we had had such a lovely conversation earlier. And — and I couldn't help but think this was deliciously ironic — I had grown quite tired from over-thinking.

I did get up to look outside over the valley outside of the front of the house and, funnily, it seemed I could see further in the night than I could earlier in the day. The light of the moon shone over the landscape and there was no fog, no mist to speak of.

It was a spectacular view, of that there was no doubt, and I, the new owner of Tŷ Glo, was the only one fortunate enough at that moment to witness it. Amidst all the isolation which served to unsettle me so, I found great comfort in that, and with renewed satisfaction, I closed the curtains and made for my bed. Funny — as soon as my head hit the pillow, I must have fallen asleep.

I wasn't aware of the time when I heard a loud yell which woke me with a start. In those first few seconds I struggled to understand what had caused me to wake, but I felt my feet, all of a sudden, go unusually, deathly cold, as if someone had just pulled up the sheets.

I sat up, startled. At first, I was unsure if it was a nightmare. Either way, I was immediately wide awake, and it was still dark outside, as if I hadn't been asleep at all. I thought of looking down at my watch and it was then I realised that every single hair on the back of my neck and arms was on end. I was confused, trying to remember what, if anything, I'd dreamed of, what had been so terrible to have woken me in such a state.

Everything was quiet — there was no light, no sound. Nothing that could explain what I was sure was a yell of some sort that woke me. What kind of yell, I couldn't describe, because I wasn't even sure if I could recall it from my semi-conscious arousal. But I was quite panicked to feel this way and not be able to explain it. I knew I had been unsettled, but to the extent I had suffered a nightmare? What else could it have been, though? And really, I was not one to believe that just because there may have been moments where I had felt unsure, the nightmare, if I had indeed had one, was a logical consequence. Either way, it was not present in my mind, so there should have been no reason for it to return into my subconscious if I were to fall back to sleep. I laid back down, still listening, but could hear nothing.

I began to drift away when suddenly I heard it again. 'MUMMY!'

It was clear as anything. A boy's call for his mother, as audible as if he were stood right next to me, as if I myself had been the one to scream. There could be no mistaking that — surely — even as tired as I was. The call hadn't been pained, or accompanied by any cry or scream. I looked around — of course, there was nobody in the room. I pushed myself out of bed and pulled back the curtain. I don't know what I expected to see, but I expected to see something, something that would explain what I had heard. But there was nothing. The hills were as clear as they had been earlier. I looked at my watch, and saw that the time was 12:30am. I looked back up, fixing my eyes slowly and carefully across the panoramic view.

Nothing.

But there had to be some explanation.

All of a sudden the strangest feeling washed over me. One of anticipation... As if I were late for an event. As if I suddenly expected the presence of a number of people... as if I were surrounded. My calves impulsively stiffened and my chest grew warm as I tried to understand this chemical change within myself. No, it wasn't anticipation, it was another sense of awareness.

I had a feeling of warmness pull on my cheeks and then a shiver which went all the way down my spine. I couldn't comprehend what I was feeling until I tried to move a step and felt a compulsion to move as quickly as possible.

I felt as if I were stood in the middle of a motorway, or, Piccadilly; I was overcome with the anxiety which comes with standing in the middle of a busy intersection — like I was somehow avoiding traffic. Moreover, I felt in the way of danger. And, even, surrounded. But, looking around myself, I was as alone as I could be. The most isolated I had been in my entire life.

As if to compound the threat of danger, I heard this shrill scream which was so high pitched that I mistook it for that of a woman yelling in terror, until I realised that in fact it was a crow, or, a red-tailed hawk. Aside from the initial shock that I was given — that understandable knee-jerk reaction of fear — I was, in fact, quite relieved.

Not so much by the sound, that would be absurd, but more, I had been scared by a very normal occurrence, that most typical of things to make you jump, and so, too tired to entertain the notion of pontificating over what these different sensations in my body could mean, I was able to rationalise what I knew to be fact. It could be explained. Birds scream occasionally.

Out here, in the middle of nowhere, with no-one around me, I had been simply been scared of the dark. I could laugh it off. Being startled, I now felt a little more awake, or at least, full of some adrenaline or nervous energy I needed to burn off.

I left the bedroom and walked towards the back, to the guest room I had been in earlier. As I got closer I could hear something, some sort of noise, although I was unable to understand what it was. Had the box I placed on the bed fallen off — was that what I had heard? I entered the room gingerly, and noticed everything was how I had left it. No, the noise was coming from behind, from outside. I moved towards the window with some hesitation. As I looked out over the back of the house, I could make out shapes, shapes around the back of what I had thought was the chapel. I attempted to focus my eyes but it was more difficult without the aid of the moonlight. I could hear water — the splashing of water — and the noises appeared to be that of human voices. I tried to open the window but it was fixed shut. A job for tomorrow. I pressed my face against the window and could just about make out for certain that it was a bunch of people moving around quickly, as if trying to catch or avoid each other.

The human mind and the dark can be a curious combination and I felt cross with myself that I'd allowed myself to be tricked. I moved quite confidently down the stairs, grabbing and wearing my coat, moving towards the kitchen and the back door before walking outside — embracing what had turned into undoubtedly the coldest temperature I had ever felt on my skin — and marching towards these trespassers. My fear — and I admit that it was — had been replaced by anger. Ostensibly I was cross because of the unauthorised access to my land but I knew to myself that my annoyance was based purely and simply on the fact that I had been caused to feel afraid in my own home and now, I felt rather foolish for having done so.

The group had stopped their manic movement the second I turned on the kitchen light and they seemed frozen to the spot. As I approached, I considered that they probably felt that nobody was home, and we were all as equally shocked by the presence of the other.

As I reached the gravestones I was now easily able to see that it was a small group of four teenagers — no older than fifteen or sixteen — who had set up some tents by the edge of the water. Two boys and two girls who seemed absolutely terrified of this figure approaching them — I hadn't considered myself to be menacing in the slightest and it thawed my anger. They were just kids.

'We're sorry, sir... we're really sorry,' said one of the boys.

'Honestly, we didn't even know anyone lived here. Nobody has lived here for years... have you just moved in?' said one of the girls, perhaps interjecting because it was less likely the person who caught them would explode with rage at a young girl.

'Yes... yes, I moved here today. What are you doing here?'

'We come here every couple of weeks to camp. It's just something we do.'

'But how did you...?' I looked around — there were no bikes, no car. I even caught myself looking to see if there was a small boat even though it would surely defy gravity for them to have scaled the hill. I could be forgiven for not thinking perfectly straight.

'We walked,' replied the first boy, more confidently now he felt re-assured I wasn't about to fly off of the handle.

'From... Dyffryn Du?' It took me a while to remember. I wasn't sure I knew how to pronounce it properly.

They all nodded affirmatively.

'But that's so far... and it's so cold. Do your parents know you're out here?'

'My parents think I'm at his,' said the talkative boy. 'And theirs think we're at mine.'

I considered the best possible recourse. Of course I could understand why they had come out here — and they were kids, I could not hold on to any anger. I was quite relieved, if the truth were to be told, of the company.

'You can't stay out here all night,' I insisted. 'Do you want to come inside? There's room.'

'We like it out here,' the boy maintained.

I was too tired to argue. But I was also in some desperate need of sleep and did not wish to be disturbed.

'Okay... just this once. But in future, please ask before you come to stay out here. It really is very cold and I would much rather not be in a position to explain to your parents. I am going to sleep now... if you must, if there is any trouble, then do knock,' I advised the youngsters before turning back to head to the house to a chorus of 'thank yous'.

'Oh, before I leave you,' I stopped myself. 'You say you walked here, did you walk around the front of the house?'

'Yes, up the hill, that's the only way here.'

'Did any of you scream? Were any of you yelling?'

'I don't think so...,' trailed the girl. 'We may have. We're really sorry if we did. We didn't mean to wake you. We didn't know, honest.'

I was able to accept that explanation. It was something my intelligence found easy to rationalise. Though I had been certain that the cry had come from inside the house, and a much later time than the group would have been making their way there from the front of the house, I also questioned my own state of mind as I knew I had become very tired, and tired people can jump to the most illogical of conclusions. Maybe, it had been the last moment of a nightmare that I couldn't remember.

I left the teenagers to their makeshift campsite and I imagined that they must have felt some reassurance that beyond the fear of the wilderness there was some safety close by. I returned to my bedroom and began to sleep until I was woken again by another noise. I could not quite make out what this noise was so I sat up and listened keenly. It sounded like a scratching, a scratching noise coming from within the house. It then stopped, and I dismissed it as just one of those sounds you expect to hear in an old house.

I laid back down and closed my eyes but the scratching instantly resumed. I waited for it to stop and it did so.

Then, soon after, it began again, and, having already once been agitated in the night, I could not really gain any sort of rest, so I got out of bed and opened the bedroom door. I stopped at the doorway and waited to hear the scratching, and the direction of it, but it did not return. That is, until I was just about to turn back in to the room, the scratching started again, and this time I was able to tell that it was coming from the room at the end of the hall.

I waited again, first for the sound to stop, and then to resume, and it did so. As I walked along the hallway I was able to tell that the scratch was more of a shuffle and sounded like something being dragged along the floor. I approached the room and went to twist the handle when I realised it was locked, or jammed. I could not get inside, try as I might. I gave up, and listened, but the scratching or shuffling had stopped.

I stood there for a while and waited to hear but it did not resume. I thought that it must be an animal trapped inside the room but I wasn't about to go to great lengths to try and open it at this late hour, so I walked back towards my bedroom, stopping briefly to go into the smaller bedroom and look out over on the young teenagers again. I could not make them out but there was no movement I could see against the dark backdrop and I could just about make out the shape of the tent.

I went back to my bedroom and, after some time, I was able to get back to a proper sleep until morning.

CHAPTER SEVEN
The Chapel

I AWOKE with the disillusion one often does after a night in a new place. My state of confusion led me to wonder whether the last two days had been but a dream. My surroundings confirmed that they hadn't, although how much of the previous night had, I was unable to determine.

Once I had got my bearings enough to remember the young teenagers outside, I rose and walked to go and check on them. I entered the small bedroom and approached the window, peering outside. It was a most beautiful morning, and with the absence of fog, mist, or any poor weather, the uninterrupted view over the back of the house was remarkable. The teenagers, however, were gone. Not even a suggestion that they had been there at all.

I checked my watch to see that it was 8:06am. I had had a decent sleep. Perhaps the youngsters had woke at sunrise and decided to make a move. I ventured over back to the master bedroom and looked towards 'The 'Snake' and there I could just about make out in the distance, four figures disappearing into the horizon. It must have been their movement which disturbed me into waking, though I didn't mind. They had seemed most respectful once aware of my presence and also seemed respectful of the land itself.

Such had been my amazement and wonder at what I did see, that I realised there was much of the house I hadn't viewed yet. It was in this moment that I remembered that the master bedroom had an en-suite and I felt such a fool — I was able to prepare myself for the day sufficiently in there, refreshed to discover the water was running and it was running warm.

After getting ready and dressed I went downstairs to sort out breakfast. Lillian had packed more sandwiches — I picked some simple cheese sandwiches — and a small assortment of fruit, so I treated myself to an apple. Tea and milk were also provided although I had not searched to find a kettle and I certainly hadn't brought one with me. I instead looked through the cupboards to find a glass or cup for the milk and found plenty of cutlery and crockery. As I sat at the table with my small breakfast I felt a little like 'Goldilocks' — my excitement the previous day had included all the thoughts of being the owner of the house although today, or at least this morning, I felt more like a guest. I felt that when Clara arrived — hopefully tomorrow — it would feel more like home.

Although I had the desire to see more of the house, after eating, I did instead go to the library to call Hector as I felt it was a more appropriate time to discuss bringing some wood for the fire. He said that I would be better served going into the village as his car wasn't really equipped for the transportation of heavy goods and I quite agreed with him.

He did say that he and Lillian would come over later, and that they would bring dinner. I was most grateful and, upon ending the telephone call, I gathered up my coat and made for the door. I paused for a moment, sure I'd forgotten something, but then realised, what else did I have? What more did I require on my person? I had warmth and money.

I exited and locked up, looking out over the stateliness of the setting. Ensuring I was wrapped up warm, I began my stroll towards the pathway that followed into the narrow road down the hill. Then, the feeling of having forgotten something niggled at me again. No, it was more than that — it was a presence. I felt a cold chill on the back of my neck that caught me so much by surprise that it provoked me to turn around. I was bewildered as there was nothing at eye level — it was only when the flash of movement of an object, of something, in the master bedroom window, made me refocus the direction of my gaze. It appeared to be a figure, a man, although I had not managed to get a proper look.

I raced back inside the house to confront the intruder. I anxiously unlocked the door, messing with the keys, and got inside.

'Hello — who's there?!' I shouted from the hallway, as I begun my ascent up the stairs. I quickly glanced around the lower level as I walked up, to see if I'd missed anything, before fixating myself with the master bedroom. The door was open — I went inside, but it seemed much as I had left it. Nobody was inside. I checked the en suite but it was empty.

Moving back into the hallway, I went to the second bedroom, the guest bedroom I'd now become familiar with, but it too was empty, just as I'd left it this morning. The separate bathroom was empty too. Where could the person have gone? I then went one by one through the upstairs rooms I had yet to go through, first of all, another bedroom — another guest room, just as welcoming as the other. Then, another smaller bedroom, which, although it could easily be served and presented as a double, was not quite as impressive.

I had not paid due attention to the presentation as I was far more concerned with finding the invader and I had convinced myself that whoever he (or she — I had not got a clear view) was was bound to be in the final room I had yet to open, at the end of the upstairs landing. The room that I had been certain I had heard the scratching from in the middle of the night.

I advanced slowly towards the door and twisted the door handle. I did not know if I expected it to open but if it did I was fully braced for some sort of confrontation. Mindful of my impression that there was some animal in there, and expecting something or somebody may jump or move quite quickly, I carefully edged the door open. It opened quite easily. I walked inside and scanned the room, which seemed as if it might have been a workspace. There were large items covered with white sheets. I pulled them off to reveal life size mannequins, and, with much more of the room visible now the sheets were away, I was able to see a large sewing machine. It looked immaculately kept. In fact, if I were a casual visitor to the house (and I wasn't far off that) then I would probably have assumed that this room had been given more care than the others. Aside from the library, this was the only room that appeared to have more than just the basic furnishings, it was filled with these personal possessions that suggested some true personality, adding colour to the lives of the previous occupants.

'Hello?' I asked, to the sound of silence.

I backed out of the room and looked again down into the hallway.

'Hello?!' I repeated, meekly, and at this point not even expecting a response.

My thought returned to the teenagers — had I seen all of them? Maybe one was remaining. Still, I had been awake and moving around for a long enough while to have noticed a disturbance or sound outside. It just didn't make sense. I thought back to the sound I had heard which had woken me with a start, what I had taken to be the sound of a young boy. Flummoxed, I walked back in the work room. No, I could explain the confusion of the last night. I couldn't explain this. I once more looked around the room and once more saw nothing. I walked over to the window which overlooked the side of the house and could see nothing of any note outside, just the miles of valley and country.

I approached the window overlooking the back of the house and scanned the horizon from right to left. And then I saw, amongst the rows of what I had imagined were once pews, a figure, as if the lone attendee at a funeral. I could hardly believe my eyes — the figure appeared to be sat, but I had been there just yesterday and could clearly see there was nowhere to sit other than on top of the stone itself. I watched the figure for a few moments and it remained still, unmoving. Knowing as I did that there was no way that he or she could be sat, I grew unnerved. Once again emboldened by the fact I now knew I was dealing with a real being rather than... well, to be perfectly frank, I don't know, but the known is always easier to comprehend than the unknown, but anyway, I was able to summon the courage rather easily to go and confront this figure.

The walk down the stairs and through the kitchen gave enough time for my anger to dissipate. I thought of how I'd approached the youngsters last night, that they had appeared more scared of me, and I thought of a logical reason why this person may be here. I knew nothing of the history of Tŷ Glo, perhaps this was a relative of the Roberts family who had come to pay their respects after learning that the house was no longer in the family? I should be reasonable. I walked through the kitchen and left the house but as I did so, I noticed that the figure was no longer at the pew.

The air was clear yet there was this lingering obstruction. It wasn't mist, cloud, but instead, the optical trick that I can only describe as the way petrol fumes obscure vision, as if your line of sight is blurry. It had such an impact that my immediate reaction was to smell for petrol or fuel, but there was no aroma or scent, only the wet of the morning dew. Confused further still, I walked closer to the chapel, and saw that the figure — a man — was there, but now stood some distance behind, by the edge of the stream, and had momentarily been obscured by my line of sight. I appeared to have walked through the 'haze'.

Though I wasn't sure who the figure was I was now able to at least determine that it wasn't one of the teenagers and that, as I had reckoned, stood where he was, he was there to pay his respects, or apparently so. But as I got closer, I saw he had set up a fishing rod, though he wasn't holding it, he was instead stood, motionless.

'Hello? Can I help you? My name is Finn, Finn Harper, the new owner,' I enquired as I walked closer.

The man turned to face me but said nothing.

As he did so, my shoulders felt such a sharp sense of cold

that it sent a shiver shooting down my spine and caused my head to jerk involuntarily. It felt as if, not only was I faced with this man, but that I was surrounded by others, and that feeling caused me to look about myself, but I could see nobody, and I drew back to look back at the man.

I was given a startling shock by his appearance — he seemed poorly, that was the only way I could think to describe his peculiar image; and, quite afflicted by his illness, to the point that he was older than his face seemed to suggest. Yet, there was a kindness and a withdrawn smile on his face, the kind which acknowledges your sympathy, though I wasn't aware that such an emotion was evident from my expression. I had frozen to the spot some way before the chapel because I almost felt I was the intruder, imposing on the personal space of this poor person.

'Hello, can I...?' I asked again.

I was cut off by him properly lifting his head to look at me. The feeling returned, that cold, horrible freeze in my shoulders. Our eyes met concomitantly, mine reluctantly yet willing, and his the same. It was a reluctant acknowledgement of the existence of each other. If I were to be truthful I most expected some kind of sorrowful glaze to his eyes but it could not be further from the truth. This man looked nothing like my father but the glare he gave me was this look of disappointment that was unmistakably that of a father disapproving of the actions of his son. As if I had committed some grave atrocity and, shamefully, I allowed this feeling to overcome me.

I opened my mouth to speak but did not know what to say, and as I did so, his expression changed slightly, his eyes sharpening, as if both waiting for my next words, and yet at the same time, warning me that I shouldn't. In fact, this subtle change felt like a warning that I should leave, and leave now. I saw his hand move. It was ever-so-slightly, but I saw the glistening of a knife. I turned quite suddenly upon my heels, and I retreated quickly to the house, to the kitchen, slamming and locking the door behind me and finding myself struggling for breath. I was surprised to find I was quite close to tears.

Unable to compose myself or think reasonably, I raced towards the front door, opening and then locking it behind me, quickly looking across the valley and seeing nothing. Determined, I moved forward, towards 'The Snake', too frightened and feared to look backwards, motivated to move faster by sheer adrenalin, moving faster as I careered down the hill, all the while trying to maintain the composure and stability towards my left so that I didn't fall over and down the steep hill. Once I was at the bottom, that adrenalin was still running through my veins and made me run and run.

I did not stop until I reached the village.

Chapter Eight
The Appleton Brothers

FOR ONE so prone to over-thinking and procrastinating there was at least a complete clarity in my mind about moving swiftly away from the house. I had questions — of course I did — but my natural state of response had drawn me to jump to conclusions and presumptions in the time it took me to get to Dyffryn Du on foot. It all made sense.

The man must have been a squatter, a homeless; the Appleton's must have been aware of his presence there and felt it easier to pass the problem on. He had been most unpleasant and my brief encounter with him had left me so unreasonably petrified that I could not, for a second, question anybody else's right to have responded in the same manner. Had he been a relative of the Roberts'? Was there another explanation for the way he seemed determined to frighten me away? Was he even trying to do that? Did he intentionally warn me with the knife, or had I misunderstood and panicked? There was a friendliness to his face, a familiarity which made him appear approachable, had I simply just reacted in haste? I could not imagine being the one given the unenviable task of attempting to evict or remove him from the premises.

It was almost enough to make somebody, anybody, feel more than just a smidgeon of sympathy, but then there was this vindictiveness that came in the last moment of our shared glance which made me apprehensive to feel such a way. No, I could not feel sympathy, even if that was against my natural reaction as a human, to feel compassion to a fellow person. Our confrontation had left me feeling disturbed, and he had used our status as strangers as an advantage in order to make me feel the way I did and achieve the power he had over me.

By the time I reached the village, my anger had become re-directed towards the people who had sold me the house rather than the man who appeared to squat there. Haunted, indeed!

But at least Hector had the common decency to inform me of what he knew of the reputation of the house. Those involved in the selling must have been there, must have been aware of this man; had they not performed a monumentally significant derelict of duty to not inform me of the trouble I might, nay, should, expect to face? Or had they thought because Clara and I were not local, much less familiar, that it would be humorous to trick and deceive us in this fashion? I certainly did not find it funny.

However, I was unsure as to how I should direct this anger. I had a very practical purpose for going into the village and so, as my most near neighbours, I did not wish to alienate anyone before Clara had even arrived. Still, if most people in the village were acquainted with this James Appleton, then I should find an answer relatively quickly.

I went straight to the White Horse — as the only public house I remembered passing with Hector, I thought it best to start there — and I was fairly fortunate to find it open at all, as it had only just turned 11am, which meant it must have taken me a good hour at least to have raced from the house. As I walked inside the open door to the lounge, I found what I assumed to be the landlord removing the chairs from the tables in preparation for his first customers of the day. I coughed so as to get his attention.

'Oh hello,' he said, turning to face me, with something of a surprised look. 'How can I help?' he asked, recognising that I was not a familiar face. For that matter, his accent — one I made out as Northern, but could not discern whether it was Yorkshire or Lancashire — marked him out as someone who may well be unfamiliar to the area. He was a damn sight more familiar to it than I was.

'Well I have a couple of queries as a matter of fact,' I responded.

'Go on.'

'I was wondering where I might find some firewood. And also where I might find James Appleton.'

'Happens I can help you on both those matters,' said the publican. 'Would you help me with the rest of these?'

'Ok, that's great,' I replied, obliging to assist moving the remaining stools from the tables. He continued to talk.

'We've lots of firewood around the back. I can have it moved for you too... as for James, well he's my brother,' said the man, pulling down the last stool and moving towards me to extend his hand. 'I'm Paul, pleasure to meet you.'

'Likewise, and I'm Finn...' I attempted to respond but Paul dismissed me knowingly.

'Yes, yes, you've bought the house...'

Of course, something I was learning quickly was that my

unfamiliarity made me stick out almost like a sore thumb. Everyone was aware of who I was.

'Would you like a drink? A cup of tea?'

At home I never considered myself a drinker. Since I'd stepped foot off of the train I struggled to think of an occasion where the liquid I'd consumed hadn't contained alcohol — maybe the first breakfast at the Percy Arms. I felt no shame in requesting a large brandy as I was still quite shaken.

'Sure,' said Paul, hesitantly. 'Hope you won't be offended if I don't join you. I have to make it through the day, after all.'

'Yes,' I said, almost to myself. 'Me too.'

With that, Paul went behind the bar to fix the drinks and also used the telephone to call James and inform him I was asking after him. After hanging up the receiver Paul let me know James would be half an hour or so.

He brought the drinks over and by way of properly breaking the ice, now I knew he was a central part of this community, I asked him about the Roberts family, and said how I'd heard from Hector that this village was essentially now run by the Appleton's.

'I suppose you could say that but we're a pleasant lot,' Paul insisted. 'I know a lot of people don't really like the way that James went about how he went about things, but the reality is that a lot of people would do what he did in his situation?'

'In his situation...?'

'Well... he came into a lot of money. Through... well... to put it bluntly, gambling. And through gambling, he made a lot more from people's debts,' admitted Paul. 'It goes without saying that it was a huge blessing to have the money but a lot of people who lived nearby were quite resentful. I could understand how some of them would be. A lot of people lost out through their own foolishness and they blamed James. James thought long and hard about what to do with the money but... well, I don't want to go too much into it, saves for what everyone around here would know and tell you, but he decided to move away from where we lived.'

'I'm not quite sure I follow what that has to do with Mr and Mrs Roberts...'

'Well, it was a matter of timing... and quite coincidental that our aunt died just as James was making that decision. And he had always been the favourite, so, his life being what it is, he inherited their house, the jammy bugger.'

I looked at Paul and I confess it must have been a strange look as I didn't quite understand how he could associate the death of a relative and luck in the same sentence. It was a look he at least understood how to respond to.

'Oh, don't get me wrong now, James kept up appearances and if he was the favourite then he had done enough to justify why, expensive birthday gifts and the like, nice bottles of wine when he went to visit, but it all fell nicely into place for him.'

'If that is so then why didn't he stay in Tŷ Glo?'

'Because he'd inherited their house too! And he'd been up there enough times to be told about the legend of that place. Better left alone.'

'So why did he sell it?'

'Isn't that what you want to ask him?'

'Yes, I guess so.'

'Anyway, I'd like to ask you a couple of questions,' Paul turned the tables unexpectedly.

'Yes, certainly...'

'You live at Tŷ Glo... you arrive here looking white as a ghost, and ask me for a large drink...'

'Please, if you wish to ask a question, please ask it directly.'

Paul looked at me studiously, as if deciding the best way to ask the question. Finally, he opened his mouth, as if he had internally practically exhausted all the different possibilities in which he could approach the topic.

'Did you see him?'

'Him? Should I take it to mean you're asking if I saw a man up at the house?'

Paul's eyebrows arched, with his expression offering nothing else in the way of confirmation.

'I saw a man, though I don't know if I can say it's the man you think of. I would guess it's the same. He left the impression... he made me feel as if I were trespassing on his property.'

'Did he scare you?' Paul's tone had changed from genuinely inquisitive to almost goading in that emasculating way men often do. His lips had curved into something of a smile that he was trying to hide.

'Well, I'm not too proud to admit so,' I said defensively. 'Anybody would have been... I don't know if scared is the right word. But I was intimidated. I would hazard a guess that the reputation of the place is why you're asking. You've never been?'

'I've no cause to,' Paul said, perhaps even more defensively than I had been.

'I didn't mean any offence,' I said with honesty. 'I don't know if I was more frightened because I'd been led to believe I should be. I concede I moved rather quickly when I saw him but I feel some regret now, some pity for the poor soul, perhaps everybody reacts that way. I'm sure he is well aware of the impression he portrays but he also looked unwell. I imagine I would be terribly alarmed if I were desperately ill and people reacted the way I did...'

'Then why don't you go back?'

'I will,' I found myself saying. I think the path of the conversation, and the realisation that Paul was scared, made me feel a little braver in myself. 'And if I see him I shall ask him if he is okay. I feel embarrassed that I reacted in the manner I did, if I'm to be honest. But when you're out here and you know nobody, well, the imagination can do something altogether unexpected to your stream of consciousness... to how rational you act in the moment... You can react as if you believe in the old wives' tale.'

I took a big drink of the brandy I had been nursing, remembering, vividly, the personal hatred emanating from the eyes of the man. And the brief glimpse of the knife. 'I don't blame anybody for not going up there if that is what has been awaiting them.'

There was a pregnant silence. I felt as if Paul had received a more bleak answer than he had been prepared for. As if he had expected me to laugh uproariously at his observations, but had also appreciated the truthfulness of my words. I hadn't sought to scare him in return and, observing his quiet, I wondered if that had unsettled him. I raised my glass, about to ask for a small top up, and Paul stopped me with his hand — I almost felt he was going to tell me not to, but he didn't. 'Don't worry. I'll get this.'

Sure enough, he topped up my glass, although he still kept his own cup of tea.

Realising that small talk would have represented a significant plummet from the point we had just discussed, Paul picked up his cup and made his way to the bar, scrubbing with a cloth although I got the impression that was more for the convenience of having something to do, to avoid the awkwardness of continuing the conversation we had.

Thankfully it wasn't too long until a man walked in who I rightfully assumed to be James, due to his physical similarity to Paul. After acknowledging his brother with a quick conversation that wasn't audible to me even if I had cared to eavesdrop, he sat beside me, taking off and dusting his flat farmer's cap before holding out his hand to greet me. He was every inch the farmer but looked as if he had dressed for the part.

'How do, I'm James, you must be Finn,' he said in the same friendly accent as his brother.

'Nice to meet you,' I said, honestly enough, although inwardly I was preparing myself to go over the unpleasantness of the conversation I'd just had with Paul once again.

'I hear you might need some firewood,' he said.

'Well, yes... although when I got to the house it did seem as if the supply would be fairly handsome. And I wonder if I should be using coal instead.'

'First of all, I wouldn't recommend using wood in a coal fire... I had a *time* selling that house, and I don't mind admitting that to you, because I know you've seen it, and I know you know what a bargain you've now got yourself.'

'Well, yes, but...'

'...and I had to figure out how best to ensure I didn't end

up out of pocket,' James continued, interrupting my own thought. I didn't think to interject that he was far from out of pocket.

'So I knew I would be selling the house and everything that was in it. It's a tough market for sellers and buyers. I decided to do something that might help both of us out.'

'Quite the illusion.'

'Oh, no, there's no illusion. It's perfectly real,' said James, looking me square in the eye. For a second, I didn't know what, exactly, we were referencing. 'I thought it would do everyone a favour if we gave a clearer view for the house by removing the trees and, then, provided a thriving business opportunity for someone in the village.'

'The village,' I responded, biting my tongue at the point I wish I'd said '*Your* village'.

'It shouldn't take too much time to cultivate a supply, and it was necessary in order to get the price down to get a buyer.'

'About that...' I replied, spurred with bravery at having already had a drink, 'why was the price so low?'

James thought before responding, 'Well, there's this reputation...' before Paul coughed, purposefully, to interrupt him. James looked at Paul but, in the circumstances, Paul looked at him back as if to say I could not be fooled.

'You've stayed there,' James said, with his intonation not quite making it clear if it was a question or a statement.

'Yes, I have,' I replied, for clarity.

There was a moment where we exchanged a glance, him not knowing whether I was aware of 'the legend', the man, and me not knowing whether to tell him I was, although I deduced it was pointless trying to pretend otherwise. I wondered if every encounter in the village might be so painful, trying to decipher whether somebody was trying to pull the wool over your eyes, before supposing it was a decidedly small population and that these experiences were likely to be one-off's.

'And, as I said to Paul, I have seen the man on the premises, the man who appears quite angry that I am there,' I said.

'All I can tell you, Finn,' James said, looking me directly in the eye, 'is that as far as I am aware, the man you say you have seen... well, I'm not quite sure how to say it, other than to say it is a trick of the imagination.'

'No, no, I can assure you, he was very real,' I insisted, with some passion, before looking at James and realising that the conviction of my performance barely mattered. It seemed as if to James and Paul, as real as this man may well have been, or seemed, they were not prepared to pay attention, even if they were willing to cajole. I must admit, though, that the conviction in his voice did catch me off guard. It was enough to make me think.

'Look, I must say, there were a group of young teenagers at the house last night, they stayed on the land, there were two girls and two boys. They were from the village and they camped at the house.' I said. I hoped that by putting somebody they might recognise into the picture that they might treat the situation with a little more seriousness.

From his position — pretending to clean glasses but more eavesdropping on our conversation — Paul interrupted.

'You know that Lauren and Macy were probably up there,' he said, knowingly, to James.

'No, they were at Oliver's,' James retorted, with the intent to dismiss and move the conversation on.

'I can't say I know the names but there were two girls and two boys at the house. They said they were from Dyffryn Du.' I clarified, to a laugh from Paul, as if he found it funny James would have to deal with his girls later on. 'To me,' I continued, 'I can only say that I saw the man, and I saw him as real as I see you. And I can repeat what I said to Paul, that he really was intimidating. What bothers me is that there is clearly a reputation attached to the house, about it being haunted, or whatever... and I have to wonder if I have been victim to some elaborate set up determined to prevent me from moving in. Or to scare me into selling up before we've even made a home.'

As I recited the words I heard them myself and grew frustrated with the potential of someone having manipulated a deception to the extent that I might be convinced to give up my house as soon as I'd stepped foot in it. I wasn't altogether sure that Paul, with his flippant attitude, may not be partly responsible and as such, it stood to reason James may be implicated too, so my suspicious nature caused me to terminate the conversation at that point, even though James protested.

'Don't be ridiculous,' he said. 'I am unable to tell you anything other than what we know and what we know is that our aunt and uncle bought the house in 1921. I can tell you to the best of my knowledge, they allowed a family or two to live there but it's been unoccupied since around the war. If what you say is true, and there have been people there... look, how can we stop people going up there? It has its reputation. If kids want to go out there and tell ghost stories... if kids want to go out there and try and scare people... kids will be kids.'

'With all due respect, I'm far from a child, and I know what I saw,' I repeated, firmly.

'I'll tell you what I will do,' said James. 'If you would like to choose how much wood you would like to take over to the house, I shall take it and you back over there and I'll go around the house with you.'

I respected James' serious offer and accepted — though what either of us were to do should we encounter the man, I was unsure. I was equally uncertain what I would actually want him to do. Confront him? I imagined he would behave in the same manner whoever he saw, if this wasn't in fact some set up. And I did feel a little uneasy about introducing a man to another who I was sure carried a weapon, even if it was the man who sold me the house.

The more I thought about it, the more I felt silly that I had been scared away. I thought about how far I ought to take it and how I might explain it to the police, if it got that far. He was an old man. He looked ill. It was probably a knife for fishing. To an objective outsider I may appear highly strung and prone to over-reaction, eager to inform the authorities at the first sign of any trouble. What good would that do for our integration into the community?

And, whatever the explanation for the presence of this man, I felt that the reaction of the brothers was enough to assume that he wasn't a local, or known to locals. After all, this was too small a village for someone of such distinguishable features to pass unnoticed. You couldn't pretend that he didn't exist.

James led me outside, around the back of the pub, to where there was a vast supply of wood piled up. He backed his small van up to a suitable area where it wouldn't prove too strenuous to load the cargo.

It didn't take long for both of us to get what James' reckoned would be at least a fortnight's worth of fuel on to his van, and then we got in and begun the journey back to 'The Snake' and beyond. It was not a journey I was looking forward to, even with the promise of good company to come in a short while.

After all, it wouldn't be too long until I was alone again, and despite the comfort of warmth I would enjoy, I had begun to feel a certain amount of trepidation about being at Tŷ Glo.

Chapter Nine
Knock

THERE COULD barely be a more contrasting emotion than the one I felt ascending the hill known as 'The Snake' compared to the day before. I now dreaded it almost as much as I'd looked forward to it the previous day even though I had tried my best to convince myself that there was little, in reality, to be afraid of.

I had always been fascinated with the human condition; what causes us to behave and react in certain ways, the way in which we respond to situations in a manner society deems acceptable, and the way our past experiences influence our logical thought pattern.

This was something I was acutely aware of during the car ride with James Appleton; I was conscious not to show too much fear having proclaimed that I should have no problem at all accosting this troublesome man and that external facade went some way to steeling my nerve for real. As James talked about the mist and the clouds — my mind wandered carelessly to how he had so earnestly tried to convince me that the man I had seen wasn't real.

I found it strange how a man of logic and reason, of

obvious business acumen which demonstrated his intelligence, could be so casually dismissive of a being, and so steadfast in his insistence to me that this person did not exist. It made me curious of his intention to do so because, had he seen him in the same way I did, he would have been left in no doubt. I did not hope to ever lay eyes on him again (I was in fact now hoping it was all some big mis-understanding and I'd simply disturbed some fisherman, whether he was local or not) but I was curious to think how James, or Paul, would have tried to explain that what they saw wasn't real if he was still there.

The weather had remained clear and so the journey up the hill was quite pleasant. I considered the route, that it was the only way in or out of the land surrounding the property. It seemed a drive that James was comfortable with, as he handled the turns with far more familiarity than Hector had. It wasn't unreasonable to think that someone could get up or down without being seen by another, but it would be quite a walk over and around the fields and hills if that journey was to avoid Dyffryn Du.

We pulled up sharply in front of the house and James and I unloaded the wood, placing it near the front door. After doing so, James offered to walk around the inside of the house, and we did so, then walking around the outer perimeter also. The walk was brisk and I did feel as if it were rushed. Everything was calm, and as I left it, but there was no sign of the man I had seen, and no sign of any disturbance whatsoever.

Having done what he set out to do, James made a quick farewell and left. He did say that if I had any enquiries or needed assistance, to just go to the village or give him a call, and I was left in no doubt that it was not just a token gesture, even if this courtesy accompaniment felt as if it were more for show. I felt his relief more tangible than my own when we got around to the back of the house and nobody was there. Still, technically, he had been good to his word, and it wouldn't be too long until Hector and Lillian would be here.

I stood and watched James drive away. I waited for a short while, and then went back inside the house, taking some wood with me to make a fire in the kitchen. I had considered his advice about using coal but felt that I should go for the less expensive option.

Quite aside from the company or anything else, I was looking forward to Lillian giving me some advice on how to work everything in the kitchen. I was not exactly a modern man, having always been looked after by my mother and then my wife, but I felt that it would be appropriate to learn some culinary skills so that I might even surprise Clara when she came up. I imagined that even having a few meaningful conversations and a few laughs over dinner might give the house more warmth, that it may turn it into more like a home. It seemed funny and peculiar to me that I had this deep-lying fascination with making it somewhere we could stay. After all, aside from Hector and Lillian, I hadn't found the area completely welcoming.

After I had moved the wood I went to the library to call Clara, just on the chance that she might be home, but there was no answer. I wasn't unnecessarily concerned by this as she should be out sorting out our affairs and hopefully she would be able to do it all today and then drive up tomorrow.

I went into the sitting room where I felt I may be able to do something to make it feel more 'homely' but I was discouraged by that same thought of meddling too much with how I'd found the house.

At a loose end, I decided to go back up into the guest bedroom with the damaged floorboard and see if I could match the wood with any that James and I had brought over, but I realised on entering that the wood we had brought was not elm. Once there, however, the silver tin caught my eye again. I thought how strange that I gone to such an effort to prize it free and yet I'd discarded it almost immediately afterwards. I must have been quite distracted yesterday, or, more tired than I had realised. Stranger still, the initial allure of the tin had been in it being so unlike anything I'd ever seen, and now, it seemed completely familiar.

I picked up the box and attempted to prize it open — it was fixed shut. It felt — and weighed — like it was solid silver, decorated with a beautiful pattern inscribed into it, like a swirling wind. I felt a little bad for the makers of this wonderful item that I had been so dismissive of it as soon as I had laid hands on it. I was more than curious, now, to learn of its contents but did not want to damage the box.

To ensure it didn't escape from my thoughts again, I picked it up and took it downstairs, putting it in the kitchen, but on the walk down I continued to look at it and noticed a small keyhole. I wondered if the key had been under the floorboards too — I hadn't noticed it, but the hole was small. I placed it on the side in the kitchen and directed myself back into the library, where I had begun to grow quite comfortable, choosing a favourite seat and so on. Although there were probably far more productive things I could be doing, the fact I had grown reticent to do much at all without Clara meant that until she got here, this was the fate I'd resigned myself to. If I could just feel a proper comfort then I might start to feel as if I really were 'Lord of the Manor'.

Honestly, I would be very content if all that Clara added was that woman's touch; that and her own company of course, because when all was said and done, and when I was in a moment as peaceful and relaxing as the one I found myself in, I was able to truly appreciate the house and feel at ease with it. The occasions I had found myself unsettled, well, hopefully they were gone. I thought that at least we had frightened away the man I had seen, although quickly corrected myself, as he must have been long gone. We did not pass him and did not see him.

I couldn't envisage a scenario where he would descend the hill — it had been difficult enough for me and I was in far better shape than the old chap — and once he knew that the house was indeed to be populated and resided in, if he was watching from afar, then he must realise that his attempts to frighten would be futile. Another trick of the mind, safety in numbers. Now, I was not absolutely settled, but I managed to find myself forgetting about my concerns on a temporary basis.

I contemplated the idea of reading the book I'd started last night to entertain me for a short while when it occurred to me that there was no television in the house! Maybe that was part of the house's initial charm, that it seemed a throwback to a time that I associated with my childhood, when life was simpler, although of course it went far further back than that. If it had been unoccupied since the First World War then a whole generation could have passed, maybe even two, and all the advances in human life with it. I hadn't even seen a radio, let alone a television. There were electric switch light sockets — which I had used as second nature without a thought — and I had found them completely in keeping with the natural decor of the house.

Or I hadn't noticed, at least.

It made me wonder how much 'renovation' had taken place but, at the same time, I was also appreciative of the subtle work they had done. I rose at once to go into the kitchen and test the oven, wondering if it may be electric or connected to another power source altogether. I had heard of electric ovens but had not yet used one in London; sadly, this one did not switch on from my attempts, so I felt it better to wait until Hector and Lillian arrived.

I was restless and quite anxious to be a good host — in my state of what I suppose you could describe as myopia or single mindedness when I raced to the village earlier, I'd forgotten about matters such as this which may be important. Just one of the many reasons why Clara was so important to me, and why we worked so well as a partnership. No matter — they were sure to understand. They were, after all, bringing the dinner, so I would find it doubtful if they assumed I would lay on some form of banquet with everything minus the food.

Back in the library, I picked up the book from last night and put it straight back down, deciding instead to look through the others available to me in more detail. One of the local travel map books caught my attention and so I pulled it out and thumbed through it, ultimately deciding that perhaps my time would be spent far more resourcefully if I examined the local area. All I knew was that I had travelled through Dyffryn Du to get to Tŷ Glo and then I was relying on word of mouth and my eye-line. I must say that I found it quite entertaining looking through the pages and it was surprising to see both how close the house was to everywhere and how far it was. I guess, travelling up a hill can make it seem like a far greater distance. I observed with interest how the houses that had existed behind ours were in an almost-crescent formation, with a chapel closest to us. I reckoned that at least one of the houses must have been converted into a local store. There was very little of note, according to these maps, for the three miles or so from the back of the house, and then it wasn't too far to sand dunes, the hills, the mines and the coast.

There was of course no road at that side which made it impossible to cross or get there — unless you were to embark on an ill-advised ramble on foot on what seemed like steep and unsteady ground — but it was nonetheless interesting to find out.

Still, the maps were just like the house, a snapshot of time more than forty years ago, and who knows what could have been built between what my eye could see and the coastline in that time. When I thought about it like that, I wondered how much of my time I had considered to be resourceful was of any use at all, but at least I was somewhat more informed than before. At any rate, it seemed to be just about the only local area guide available in the library which was written and compiled in the twentieth century.

I imagined that Clara might be quite excited at the prospect of technically owning an island in the sky. We had suspected, because of the description on the listing at the auction, that it would be the case, but this confirmation was fantastic.

I was in quite high spirits and carried away with the time when I looked up and realised that Hector and Lillian would be due any minute. Despite my failure as a host I could at least set the table with the existing crockery and so I made to the kitchen and washed the plates, dishes and cutlery before arranging them accordingly. I lifted some wood into the log burner and got it fired up so that it may be fully burning by the time they got here, and I walked to the front door to look and see if they were within eyeshot. I couldn't see anything but once I opened the door I could hear Hector's motor slowly navigating towards the house around the upper bend and so I walked outside to greet them.

For the first time I felt like I was at 'home', in this situation, welcoming guests. Driving carefully, they still took a little while to get to the house and I swear that in that time it began to get darker. The sun had already set but the dark was closing in rather fast. I presumed that Hector must only just have seen me as he flashed his lights to acknowledge my presence, and I waved back.

Soon enough, they had pulled up, and exited the car to greet me.

'How are you, boyo? Settled in, eh?' said Hector, extending a friendly hand which turned into a hug.

'Oh yes, well, you know, getting there.'

'Good to see your good lady is with you!'

'...What?'

'Clara. Has she gone through to the kitchen?'

'What do you mean?' I replied, getting agitated. 'She's not here, she's in London.'

'Well, who was stood in the doorway then?'

My blood ran cold.

'Excuse me,' I stuttered, feeling terrible that I was unable to help Hector and Lillian carry anything in to the house, but I felt a compulsion to race inside.

In fact I did not feel anything to justify a feeling of guilt as regards my unhelpful behaviour, such was the speed of my impulse. I looked in the library. Nothing. I raced to the kitchen. Nobody there.

A woman? Surely not. But like Hector, I had at first been unable to tell for sure. Was the man in the house? I held the kitchen table, partly for something to grip to ease the tension, but mostly to keep me upright. My friends, by this point, had entered the kitchen.

'What's up lad? What's upset you?' said Hector.

'Oh Finn are you alright? Where's Clara?' asked Lillian, talking over her husband.

I felt as if a million fantastic burning impulses were racing through my body. A trick. Anxiety. What?

'Tell me... what did you see, who did you see?'

'Well, you know, I'm not sure,' started Lillian, slowly, un-convincingly. 'It might just have been the light, I don't know.'

'No, you said you saw Clara. Did you see Clara or did you see a woman, or a man...'

'Honestly Finn, it might... it probably was just the light. We've never been here before!' interrupted Lillian insistently.

I looked at Hector. I hoped that he would not try to brush me off with the same childish kind of dissuasion and he did not, but he did not even attempt, almost ashamedly looking down at the floor as if he did not want me to even ask.

'Hector,' I said affirmatively. 'Please come outside with me — if there is another person here then I can assure you that they are no guest of mine, and I would like to confront them. I saw a man today at the back of the house and when I came back he had gone. If he is here...'

I felt Lillian look across at Hector as if to tell him to refuse but such was the situation that he could not do so reasonably. For a second I could not tell if Lillian's objection was because she did not want to be alone or she sincerely did not want Hector to go with me.

'Come on,' I said. 'We'll go through the front and then back in through the back.'

As we left the front door, we checked down the left hand side with our eyes, before walking around the right hand side of the house, towards the chapel and the gravestones. We then looked in the shed, and tried to get a good look of the view of the house from the outside.

I looked upstairs at the back bedroom windows. Nothing. Nobody.

I would have liked, with every fibre of my being, to believe that they were being honest in their suggestion that it may just have been a trick of the light, but I knew enough to know better.

I knew that I wasn't being paranoid, and I knew that even though I hadn't seen this person, this woman... Surely it was the same man I had seen. And if it was in fact a woman, and now, I had no real reason to question the credibility of their instant reaction, then she must be connected to the man in some way.

I also knew, instantly, from the reaction of Hector and Lillian, that their reasons for responding the way they had were not rational. Or they didn't seem it. James and Paul had been quite dismissive of me earlier in the day but the reason I had wanted James out at the house with me was to judge the look on his face if he would see what I had. I was able to confirm, by the way that my friends had reacted, that my own feeling of being disconcerted was quite justified, and it instantly put me on edge.

I think, oddly enough, prior to this very moment, I had allowed myself to believe in the disbelief. I was a stranger, I was caught up in a lot of change, so if there were a few things happening around me that I found questionable, then, at least that was being dismissed as irrational by others.

But now, witnessing what I knew to be real fear in the eyes and behaviour of people I knew meant me no harm, I felt an uneasy dread overcome me. All of a sudden, the various emotions that I had felt fleetingly came at me from various angles. This man's appearances, the encounter I had with him yesterday, the look in his eyes... I don't mind admitting that all at once I felt rather sick. Hector acknowledged that and put his arm around me, much like a kindly uncle, steadying me and walking me to the door where we could access the kitchen.

There was a most awkward silence for what seemed like around four or five minutes, but may easily have been just one.

I had sat down on a seat at the table where I was able to get a good view of the outside through the window and Hector had made us all a large drink of brandy, more or less polishing the bottle off from the previous night. Lillian did try and advise him against it because of his driving but he was adamant and I wasn't about to talk him out of it. We all sat around the table, unwilling or unable to talk, nursing our drinks, thinking of a way to initiate conversation. I cannot speak for what was on either of their minds but I ran through a million things; why, what, how? They must know something more than they had let on. When it became clear that they were not going to say something, I had to.

'Who was she?' I asked, looking at both of them.

'I really don't think this is a good idea,' said Lillian. She had a more than frightened tone to her voice, almost upset, and I almost felt immediately apologetic.

Hector reached across and put his hand on hers, and it was a warmth that touched me so much that it brought tears to my eyes, although those tears were probably sitting in the ducts already, just waiting for the next emotional provocation to burst.

Another awkward silence followed and I felt reticent to break it again after last time. We had said nothing, nothing of note between us of this man or woman, whoever they were, yet it had become plainly clear this was not a conversation for now. And, for my part, I now agreed, I could not bear to see Lillian continue to be upset.

I eventually decided to cajole some spirit into the proceedings.

'Now, I know as a Londoner you may laugh at me for not quite getting the hang of things,' I began, 'but I really cannot figure out this oven. Whoever the Appleton's hired to update this place... well, they've done a grand job, but I appear to be lost in a space in time, unsure of what is an old feature and what is new, and what is somewhere in between.'

Hector looked unsure but quite relieved the tone had changed and Lillian, for her part, looked grateful I'd at least made the effort.

'Now we can't expect a strapping lad like you to know everything can we?' she said.

'Easy now!' laughed Hector.

From that moment, the shared apprehension between us

seemed to disappear, as Lillian first got up to show me how to work the oven, and then explained how we would do the washing. She was insistent that the out house would be an ideal place and I was equally stubborn that I wished to retain that for my own leisure — I knew that in time, she and Clara would get on quite well, as Clara always did with older people, empathising with their older souls and rejoicing in their greater experiences. And Lillian, like Clara, very much appeared to be the wearer of the trousers in the family, the matriarch, and the owner of a humour quite stern but loving. She did feel like a mother, and she continued to show those traits when she took over making dinner despite my best of intentions. Hector told me to just let her get on with it and so I acceded to that request and sat with him, as he proudly landed a big jug of 'home brew' ale on the table. Lillian came over and brought a couple of glasses to the table — the first taste of it was so strong that I thought another might knock me out!

Thankfully, Lillian's homemade Shepherd's pie was much more pleasing to the palate, though I must confess that I did partake in one or two more drinks of the deadly home brew. After it became more familiar, it became more tolerable, as in keeping with those very first experiences I'd had with alcohol as a teenager. At one point I pondered whether it might be worth resisting but I felt I was essentially in Rome, so it was time to do as they did.

After eating, I insisted we move into the lounge, as I felt sufficiently inebriated by Hector's potent fuel to indulge in the luxuries that I had yet to enjoy in the house and we did have a good hour in there, chattering frivolously about Hector's hopes and dreams and then my own, jovially disregarding the values of Dyffryn Du compared to Aberaernavon with their own tribal loyalty.

As they prepared to leave, Lillian went to the bathroom, and that left Hector and I sat, looking at each other. After a couple of moments he said,

'Son... we're not far away.'

'Please,' I said. 'Is there anything, anything I should know?'

'You know there are things,' he admitted. 'But, this really isn't the time or place. If you would like to come back with us you know I will gladly take you, there will always be a place...'

He left the last comment lingering in the air, waiting for a response.

'No, I should be fine,' I said.

I thought about taking him up on his offer but then I remembered how upset Lillian was and how any further talk of anything away from the routine would be an aggravation that shouldn't be appropriate to end the nice and pleasant evening that we had managed to make it.

Lillian returned from the bathroom and on her entrance we all exchanged pleasantries; she, reminding me that she had left me plenty of Shepherd's pie for the following day, and I, cheekily requesting a regular supply.

'I might be able to stretch to the recipe,' she said, giving me a warm hug.

'I will hold you to that!'

With that, they both made for the door, stopping only to give me a brief hug as they left. I stood and watched as they got into the car and begun their drive away from the house, towards the hill. I was able to see clearly into the night, and though terribly cold, it was a reminder of the most beautiful scenery we had.

I was feeling a little light headed and upon re-entering the house I discovered that Hector had left the remainder of his home brew. I thought to call Clara and then perhaps finish it off, but when I looked at my watch, I was surprised to see it had just turned midnight.

I did not consider that I was tired as I felt some invigoration from the lovely evening; I found myself still laughing at some of Hector's jokes, or rather, his opinions, as I sat back in the sitting room. Now I had seen this fantastic room used for its purpose it did not seem quite as intimidating, or daunting. I relaxed in my chair and then realised that I was, indeed, quite tired, and, I confess, inebriated after all. Still, that relaxation was very welcome, so I indulged in it a little while longer, but when I felt myself drifting off to sleep, I pushed myself to come around and get up to bed.

I imagined I must have fallen asleep instantly because I barely remembered much from the second I left the sitting room to getting into bed.

I woke again, startled by a sound. It came again rapidly, a loud banging on the door to the house. I jolted out of bed and looked out of the window. I was unable to crane my neck to see the door and so I knew I would have to go down and answer it. I looked out on to the front of the house and could see no vehicle.

BANG BANG BANG BANG.

The knocking continued with an impatience as I left the bedroom and began to nervously walk downstairs. I stopped, halfway down the stairs. I did not want to answer the door.

The knocking stopped with me. I stood there, frozen to the spot, for a minute or so, and there was no further sound.

I walked down a couple of steps and noticed that the light in the kitchen was still on. I could've sworn that I turned it off. I walked down into the kitchen and nobody was there — I looked outside and could see nobody. The light begun to flicker and so my attention was diverted towards the ceiling to look at it. Then, I heard a noise, something coming from the library, almost like a shuffle or as if someone had banged into the desk. I looked around, towards the library door from my position just inside the kitchen doorway, but saw nobody.

Suddenly, I felt a breeze on my neck, and heard a young boy say 'Daddy!' as if he were stood right behind me, trying to get my attention.

I turned, startled, and saw nobody — but now, on the table right in front of me, was the silver tin that I had found under the floorboards, open, revealing its contents. The inside of the box was cloaked with a red velvet liner and held a handful of toy soldiers, some toy farmyard animals and a small tin train.

I noticed I was breathing rather heavily and put my hand to my brow — I had worked up a panicked sweat and started to wonder if I was, in fact, losing my mind. If all of these things that I had led myself to believe were just an extreme paranoia, if I had always had some sort of propensity or vulnerability to feeling this way, and the isolation had been a trigger point.

Then, I heard the laugh of a child outside, a young boy again, as if he were running and playing freely in the dead of the night. I looked outside and could see no-one, so I ventured to the door and outside.

The laughter and running seemed further away still, near

the chapel, near the gravestones, and so I walked towards them. Yet I could still not see anyone. I turned to walk back to the house and, against the backdrop of the light of the kitchen, I saw the haze, that petrol smog, as if I had turned and left the gas on. Something within it caught my eye.

Stood in the doorway of the kitchen was a lady, obscured... created, even, by this smog, only visible by and within its deviation from the normal atmosphere. Yet I could clearly see a slight, short lady, with strong, matronly shoulders. The way she held herself gave her a presence every bit as intimidating as the man I had seen on the land earlier. Against the pitch black of night and the light behind her in the doorway her presence was deeply unsettling. I was unable to look away even though I wanted to. She looked at me with the purest of disdain, her eyes distinctive, and real, unwelcoming just as much as the man had been.

Then, she started to move towards me, separating herself from the mist which had seemed to create her, becoming more visible, more real.

My natural compulsion was to run, run as fast as I could, but my feet refused, and I wondered if I might accept whatever horrible fate I was destined for. I closed my eyes tightly, simply unable to tolerate the feeling which was emanating from the woman, and the sense that I was about to suffer some terrible injury.

BANG BANG BANG BANG.

I woke with a start, to hear the impatient knocking once more. I was in bed, in the master bedroom.

Had I gone mad? Was I delirious?

BANG BANG BANG BANG.

It was remorseless. I closed my eyes again, wondering if I might wake up safe and sound in London, next to Clara, with this all nothing but a terrible dream.

BANG BANG BANG BANG.

It continued. This was definitely real. I had grown weak and tired with my emotions and reactions in this relentless to and fro, this constant battle between logic, the absurd, and the illogical absurd reaction of everyone who I had dared to ask. I was almost too afraid to get out of bed at all, until I noticed a light outside — I summoned up the courage to get out of bed and go to the window.

I saw Hector's car.

I looked at my watch and saw that it was 2am — what ever had possessed him to come back?

I went downstairs in a hurry, answering the door. I must have looked quite the state because Hector was taken aback by what he saw.

'I knew I shouldn't have left you,' he said. 'Now, where are your clothes?' I couldn't answer, but Hector went upstairs anyway, to the master bedroom, helping himself to what he could find.

'No matter if they are clean, we'll sort that out later,' he said. 'Okay,' I replied quietly.

With that, he led me out of the house, and into his car. I did not look back.

CHAPTER TEN
Fog

WE DROVE for some distance before the usually talkative Hector was prompted into life. It gave enough time on the drive to give thought to those few moments not long after we'd bought Tŷ Glo when Clara and I laughed so dismissively at the thought of it being haunted. She had even felt it would be an attraction should we desire to turn it into a guest house but I knew for certain any business of that sort would not be attractive to locals. Both of the times I'd spent at the house, I'd ultimately ended up fleeing for safety.

The very thought of going back at all was not one I was willing to entertain at present even though I knew I must, at some point. I was quite feverish — my subconscious state of being unwell was something I felt now, as I tried to make some sense of what I'd just experienced. I knew it was a dream, a nightmare, that I had not moved from the bed, and yet I could still hear the voice of the boy, I could still picture the woman with the damning expression on her face, and, imprinted in my mind, it was as clear as when I had seen the man earlier in the day, in clear consciousness.

Normally, when I dreamt, something would be obscured,

or a person or place normally familiar to me would not be as they would be when I was awake, but that was not the case. Everything was most real and I was left under no illusion that I was an unwelcome intruder in Tŷ Glo, and not welcome to return, either.

When we were far enough away from Dyffryn Du — I might say, far enough away to be safe — Hector broke the silence.

'You know,' he said, calculating his words. 'I just had this feeling. We got back into the house and Lillian got herself ready for bed, and I just felt like I ought to come and get you.'

'Whatever the reason, I'm quite glad,' I responded. I knew I needn't explain further.

I thought for a while if Hector's decision was so out of the ordinary that I could now feel comfortable in raising the most uncomfortable of subjects, but as I tried, he simply raised his hand.

'Not now, lad. You're not thinking straight. Nor am I,' he said.

We got to Aberaernavon, and the Percy Arms, and the sight was almost as warming as my own home.

I was taken to bed and I ought to have slept a little easier but I was restless, conscious of every noise, every creak. It took some time, and I didn't feel any benefit for it, but I know that I must have slept to some extent because I remember the feeling of waking. The few seconds before full consciousness were a sanctuary before, first, the panic of what I had endured, and then second, the realisation that I was safe, after all. I was most comforted. I had a headache which may well have been owing to the alcohol, or the exhaustion and procrastination, or maybe, a combination of all.

After gathering my thoughts, my first plan was to contact Clara, tell her of my experience, and ask for what she thought would be the sensible next step. Out of protection I would be unwilling for her to even go to Tŷ Glo with me and I considered asking her whether we should seek legal advice.

In my giddiness to get the house I hadn't read through all of the small print of the contract, the error of a beginner I must admit, yet I — we — just felt it so much of a bargain that we couldn't lose. Still, as fearful as I was, I was also reluctant to give in so easily. There ought to be some logical explanation; the most logical I could think was that in spite of their protestations, this has been part of an elaborate plan by the Appleton family, and that we might be forced to sell at a loss. As much as I did not wish Clara to be subjected to the threat or harassment of the man, I also did not wish to look foolish.

At breakfast I attempted to raise the subject of the house once again. I waited until Lillian had served Hector and I, as she appeared unwilling to join us; and at a guess, I thought that she may well have expected my choice of conversation.

'Hector, I must insist that we speak about Tŷ Glo, and that you tell me what you know,' I said, sternly.

'Son, I know you've been through something... and I know that it's enough to make you believe in the stories or the whispers,' he began.

'That's the thing. What stories? What whispers? I feel like I have a right to be scared but I don't know why, and to be quite honest, I feel that it's the unknowing that is most unsettling,' I confessed.

'As I told you the other day, they say the house is haunted... I am not one for gossip as you know, so I won't fill your head with my own thoughts, as I'm sure you have enough. Until the other day, I had not set foot in that house,' he said.

I didn't answer immediately as I knew he was being honest and so didn't know how next to tackle the subject.

'There is a part of me that wants to protect you but I know that you are determined to know the truth,' Hector finally continued. 'If you really want to know... and I place some emphasis on the if... then you could go to the library in town and go through the old newspaper records. Our library is the biggest in the local area... in fact, I'm not sure Dyffryn Du has one. So anything you need to find will probably be in there.'

'Thank you Hector,' I said, honestly.

'No, don't thank me. Nothing to thank about it,' he insisted. Having done what he felt he needed to do, Hector quickly diverted the conversation to matters more flippant, boasting that he was to do very little that day.

I tried my hardest to pay attention but I could not help but feel a certain anticipation about finally finding out the truth. I wasn't relieved, but nor was I fearful, if anything, I felt in a state of limbo.

I believed that Hector wasn't withholding any information I ought to have known but I also felt that there were plenty of tales he knew of, tales I felt I might benefit from being aware of. I could appreciate what he was doing in not giving way to idle gossip. I did not mean to be ignorant to the conversation but could not help my mind from wandering. Without a shadow of a doubt, this matter was dominating my thoughts, and it would do me a world of good to place some reasoning behind it.

I walked outside and felt the cold chill in the air amid the returned fog. With the reduced visibility and bright street lights providing some sort of navigation and guidance, I could have been anywhere, though the fact I was in a small village was of some convenience when it came to the fact that I'd have to find a library.

That had been one thing I'd neglected to ask Hector as I'd pushed him enough and felt fortunate to have received the information I had. Fortunately, it wasn't so far, and my sight wasn't obscured to the point I couldn't reasonably see in front of me.

It took me only a matter of minutes to find the library and I was pleased to find it open, although inside, it was deserted save for the assistant at the front desk. I took a look around myself but my search was fruitless and so I was forced to approach the young lady at the counter.

'Excuse me, I was wondering if you could help,' I enquired.

'I hope so — that's what I'm paid for!' she quipped in return.

'I'm not entirely sure what I'm looking for. Well, no... I know what I'm looking for. Newspaper records. But I'm not sure when.'

'Do you have any kind of idea?'

'Well,' I started, wondering what kind of response I would elicit, 'anything that discusses the events of Tŷ Glo...'

Her eyebrows raised.

'Anything from, I don't know... 1890 to 1910? Whenever the ownership changed to the Roberts family. Or, really, anything. Anything that followed the war, anything that talks about the house, the land...'

'May I ask why?'

'I'd... rather not say at this point.' I felt it better to keep my counsel so I didn't risk any obstruction, though, I suspected that she may have some suspicion. Her facial expression seemed to indicate as if she may not prove too helpful but I thought quickly. 'I'm the new owner. Finn Harper. I just want to know more about it,' I said.

Her skepticism seemed to waver.

'Okay,' she relented, getting up from her desk and appearing to guide me. 'Follow me.'

She walked to some large cabinets with metal drawers, which I rightfully presumed would hold all the historical local newspapers due to their size. Once the librarian had shown me the cabinets I ought to look in for the years I'd requested, she went back to her desk, and I was left to my own devices.

I must have spent an hour or so getting nowhere until I found one dated November 2nd 1909 — it was front page news of the Aberaernavon Echo that Elfyn Roberts had died. Although interesting to read and discover that he was of such importance I learned nothing of significance to add to what I already knew.

> *He spent the last thirty five years of his life in Dyffryn Du. He leaves behind his wife Hayley and no children. In 1903, Roberts bought Tŷ Glo, a move largely welcomed by the local community who have lived in peace since.*

It was enough to tell me something, but ultimately, nothing new. I put that newspaper back and decided to go back to 1903 instead, hoping that I might find something from the year that gave more relevant information. I started from January 1st, fully aware of how potentially frustrating it may prove, and was quite surprised and satisfied when I found something on page 16 in the newspaper of January 9th.

'*Local landowner and entrepreneur Elfyn Roberts yesterday
bought the notable Tŷ Glo for an undisclosed sum. The house,
which has gained much local notoriety for alleged disturbances
and unusual occurrences, has been unoccupied for four years...*'

I decided to delve a little further back and see if I could find
anything about these disturbances yet I was unable to do so.
After I had been sat there for some time, the librarian came back
over.

'Have you found what you were looking for?' she asked.

'To an extent,' I answered. 'Are you informed, educated on
the local area?'

'On Tŷ Glo, do you mean?' she cut to the chase.

'Yes... I've... Well, I want to know about these alleged haunt-
ings. The disturbances. Am I to presume... well, I would rather
not...' I rambled.

'Yes, I think the first thing any local historian learns about
this area is the story of Tŷ Glo. If you are the owner I cannot
believe you are yet to know,' she said, suspiciously.

'I am, I can assure you. But I am not local. I've only been
in the area a matter of days. My wife and I bought the house
at auction,' I summarised. 'I've asked, but nobody appears willing to talk.'

'Parents?' she asked.

'I'm not...'

'Not you. The people you've asked.'

'That I am unable to know... well, I don't think that matters,
as I'm sure I've received evasive answers from those with or
without children,' I explained.

'Okay... well, the grounds of the house are said to be haunted by the ghost of Iris Argall and her children,' said the librarian.

'A woman... a lady. But there's a man, too.'

'Yes... that's right.'

'I did see the man. I did not see the woman but I... I dreamed. I don't know how. But I feel for sure it has to be connected.'

'I have no doubts,' she admitted. 'I cannot possibly guess what you have seen but I can... well, obviously, it is enough to bring you here.'

'Tell me. It will take me forever,' I said, frustratingly shifting papers.

'I cannot tell you what is for certain. You will not find it in there however long you look. The story goes further and beyond.'

'Surely there must be some recollection.'

'You won't find it in there,' she insisted. 'Before Iris... the house was said to have been built by a local man who lived alone. He had no family and, after the house was built, he did not marry, he had no children. When he died, it became local myth, or legend, that nobody should live there. But around the time of the industrial revolution, local men from the town thought it would be a great place to live because of how close it was to the mines and they set about building their own small hamlet.'

'Yes, the buildings...'

'That's correct... anyway... sooner or later, the men who built the houses moved in to them, and had wives of their own, and eventually families. Because of the distance of the hamlet to the nearest villages, one of the families changed their house into a convenience store, and that family — the Argall family — became wealthy, and, really, the pillars of the community. They moved into Tŷ Glo... it had been named as such, the Coal House, and the hamlet itself was named the same. Years went by, and then as the second generation became to be the workers, there was... well, it can, it was a fire you know. In the middle of the night. And it had spread between the houses before the residents could react. They did what they could but...' she trailed off. She didn't need to fill in the rest.

'The few people who survived moved away. The Argall family too, though, their house had been unscathed. It was too difficult to stay.'

'How did it come to be that one house remains, that one house and the others are ruined?'

'Well, we're still... this is still only gossip, you know,' she reminded me. 'But kids would go up there to play, to tell ghost stories. The story of the older house was that of legend. They were able to move away, were affluent enough to start over. When the boy of that family was old enough he moved back up there and knocked down the other houses. He married. They had a family, two boys. And then there were a series of events. Their first son drowned in the stream. No-one saw them after that. Then, it was the case, that so much time had passed that the people of the village were curious. So the police went up there and found the house in ruins. There was a lot of fire damage. They found two bodies... a mother... Iris Argall, and son. They had been locked inside one of the bedrooms and it seems like they were unable to get out.'

'What about the father?'

'They never found him.'

'Is that the man who roams the grounds. Is that the ghost, the man I saw, Mr Argall? Or is it the man who built the house?'

'I can't answer that. Of course, these are only local tales.'

'Forgive me but how much of those events can be said to be coincidence, just a terrible chain of events? That could have been avoided with, I don't know, proximity to police, fire services?' I interrupted.

'Well, all of it, if you lend yourself to that way of thinking,' she said, looking at me in the eyes. 'But around the turn of the century there was an unusually large number of deaths in Dyffryn Du... that's what gave it its name. The Black Valley. They blamed the house, that it was the Argall house. It was like the curse had spread to the valley. When Elfyn Roberts bought the house, nobody had cause to go. It was seen as a sacrifice for the community, and he forbade people from going up there. Because the house was uninterrupted, people just accepted that Iris and the family were in their peace, and there was no sense in going. But then Elfyn died... and then so did Hayley. And then their nephew...'

'You needn't explain about James Appleton. I'm well aware and have met him. But he has said nothing of this. In fact he said that the man is just a figment of my imagination. I dare say he would say the same about this woman too.'

'You've seen him?' the librarian looked at me with deep curiosity.

'I saw a man, an aged man who looked remarkably unwell, but fearsome at the same time. And I dreamed that I heard the voice of a child... and I saw a woman, with the intention, I'm so certain, of frightening. But I feel certain that if this, the story that you tell, is one that has circulated for generations, then it is some scheme from this James Appleton fellow to con people based on the reputation of the house,' I said. 'And the nightmare...

well... I would not give coincidence such credence normally. But...'

'Perhaps,' she replied. 'Or perhaps the house has been disturbed and so has the ghost of Iris Argall.'

'I wish to know more of the consequences. I will admit to you that I do not believe in ghosts, but if you are right in your assumption, and the man and woman I saw were apparitions, then how is that so? I am yet to hear or learn of any consequences other than my own fear, and I am growing increasingly frustrated with myself for being fooled into feeling this way,' I said, with growing abruptness. 'If all of this is just an attempt, a trick to make me scared.'

'You asked me what I knew and I can only tell you the tale,' she said in a matter-of-fact way. 'I cannot explain to you the consequences. People have died... if you want my advice, and I don't suppose you do, but I would leave the village, go to wherever your home is, and put this sorry mess out of your mind. Do not stay to wait and see what happens and do not worry yourself with the consequences.'

'Pretend they don't exist,' I said.

'Quite,' she replied. 'For some, it's too late, too futile to leave. Sometimes ignorance is bliss. If you have awaken the ghost of Iris Argall then I'm afraid, Mr Harper, you are about to become far more unwelcome around these parts than Mr Appleton himself.'

I thought about these words for a few seconds and steeled myself for my own response.

'I do not doubt the sincerity of what you say to me,' I said. 'And I do appreciate the warning. But I just cannot logically accept this explanation. No, it has to be some kind of set up. I just cannot... I will not be driven out. I won't be scared out. I really cannot thank ou enough for your help. You have shed much light on something that appeared very unclear.' I stood up from the desk and started to organise the papers.

'If you are leaving, I can do that,' she offered. 'It will at least give me something to do.'

I thanked the librarian again for her help and made to leave. My intention was to head straight for Dyffryn Du, straight to confront Paul or James, and this time, refuse to accept their explanation. I would insist that if this nuisance was to continue then I would have no hesitation in contacting the police.

I left the library and stepped out into the cold, foggy street. I did not wish to bother Hector on his day off and so I walked to the train station in the hope that I might catch a taxi cab to Dyffryn Du. There was one ready as I got there.

The fog had thickened a little and so the journey to our neighbouring village took a little longer than it had done previously. From the surroundings that were visible I could tell we had reached Dyffryn Du when we heard the most sickening thud in front of us — my driver harshly hit the brakes. We both jumped out of the motor to see what had happened and noticed a body trapped under the car in front. The driver of that car had yet to get out, probably still caught in shock.

As I got closer I noticed that the body was familiar. It was that of a teenager, a girl. In the light of day (albeit influenced by the fog) I was able to tell it was one of the girls who I had seen at the house the other night. If I considered myself familiar then that was nothing to my driver, who appeared to personally know the girl.

'Lauren, Lauren!' he shouted, shaking the girl's shoulders. She was unconscious.

Hysterical cries of 'She's bleeding!' and then 'She's not

112

breathing!' surrounded the action of the driver which was a stark contrast to my motionless, frozen pose. Lauren... one of James' daughters had that name.

'Oh my God. She's dead, she's dead!' cried the driver. 'Lauren, talk to me. Lauren, talk to me!'

She did not respond. She could not.

If what the librarian had said was true, then there was bound to be a consequence, a victim from my sightings of the man I had seen, the woman I had dreamed, the voices I had heard.

Could it be?

How could it be?

A feeling of dread washed over me in an instant. One of guilt, one of trauma, one of compassion for the loss of a young life. I clung to the side of the car and looked inside, to see the driver — an unfamiliar face — sobbing, hands on the wheel.

Was I able to tell what had happened for certain? No. But one thing I could reasonably conclude was that it was doubtful that James and his family would play God if this was the tale that resonated through the local area, and that their family was shortly to learn of the tragedy it had suffered. And if James or his family were not to blame, then the absence of a logical conclusion made me more fearful than ever.

Chapter Eleven
Going Back

THE MOMENTS which followed the accident — if that's what it was — were a blur.

James Appleton arrived on the scene and cradled his young daughter. The strong and authoritative persona and facade melted away as the reality of a man losing his child became all too apparent.

Paul Appleton followed and then what I presumed to be other family members who I had yet to become acquainted with. Paul looked at me and for a second I felt some resentment. Gone was the almost derisive or dismissive look, gone was the patronising glare, replaced by a glance that seemed to articulate that I was somehow responsible.

I was unnerved by this but partly because I was slowly realising why he felt like that, if he did. Perhaps he was angry at himself. Perhaps we were both culpable, all culpable, we all bore some responsibility for what happened. They could have told me instead of laughing me off, something should have been said before I went to the house. Maybe I should have gone as soon as I had become unsettled but how was I to know? I had got what I wanted, some explanation, some logical reason that went some way to rationalising the unusual events I had experienced, yet that explanation was in itself absurd. I had been convinced to believe in the supernatural and it was at odds with everything I had been taught, everything I had learned throughout my life.

Considering events as they were, it would be pointless confronting James as I had intended — sympathy aside, I imagine that my questions had already been answered, that neither he nor his family were responsible. If there was still a possibility that this all was some kind of ruse, then it was elaborate, vicious, and being orchestrated by somebody else.

I don't know why, but amid the uncertainty, what I felt compelled to do more than anything else was to go back to Tŷ Glo. I had belongings there that I should recover and, now being privy to the tales of this house, this unnamed and unknown man, this woman, Iris Argall, I felt more comfortable that I could deal with something I knew, even if what I did know what surreal. Of course, Iris Argall had died many, many years before, but I imagine that my knowledge of who the imposter or the intruder was imitating would unsettle them in return, and place some of the power back into my own hands. It was a feeling of control that I was keen to have and exert over my new home and land.

I was able to begin my journey to Tŷ Glo on foot as I had grown a little familiar with the journey — the road, or pathway, to 'The Snake' did not deviate once it left the village and so despite the fog I knew I would be able to navigate my way there.

Forgive me if my thoughts at this point sound callous and uncaring but my primary instinct was one of protection and I could not completely dismiss the theory that sightings of these ghosts, if the man and this imaginary woman were indeed a ghost, brought the consequence of death. I had now seen this to be true if I bought into the story and I must confess that I had felt such a multitude of contrasting emotions that I felt constantly on the brink of exhaustion and delirium, as if I was in some rancid state of living nightmare I could not shake myself from. In my brisk walk through the fog I thought of it and my mind turned to the smog, the haze, and how I'd seen it and walked through it when I'd seen the man on the land. It was the same mist, the same haze, that the woman had apparently materialised from in my nightmares. It challenged my intelligence. I had heard of ghosts. I considered myself sane. Could only I see what I did? I tried to recall if I had suffered some bump which may have impaired my vision. Something that may explain the appearance of the woman. I was of sound enough mind to challenge myself. Was this how people saw ghosts? That jump from the reasonable to the unreasonable. Was this how ghosts infiltrated the conscious mind? And, now that I had seen what I had, what other dreadful events might occur?

After a time which was shorter than I had reasoned, probably owing to the adrenalin in my veins, I reached what I knew to be the ascent of 'The Snake', the fog was so thick that I was unable to see more than ten or fifteen feet in front of me.

Fortunately, what I could see was enough to keep me on the pathway, though if I should veer ever so slightly off, I knew that the difference in solidity of the ground would be enough to steer me right.

I was quite proud of my geographical memory although I was still slightly disoriented. I was given cause to stop when I heard a noise at a bend that I figured was the final one before approaching the front of the house. It was the faintest sound of music, what I could make out to be country music, or rockabilly, hillbilly music, a song which I felt to be familiar.

The music was then drowned out by what appeared to be the sound of the patter of feet running, though I could not tell whether it was in front or behind me. Either way, I thought, it must be coming towards me, as I had not heard it until this point.

'Hello?' I shouted, looking around. 'Hello?'

There it was again. That voice, that same voice of the young boy.

'Daddy, Daddy!'

It sent a sickening chill down my spine. 'Who is it? Who's there?'

The sounds did not return and the footsteps did not pass me, so I reasoned the child must have turned back and gone to the house or its proximity.

I quickened my own pace, questioning if anyone was there, loudly. 'Who's there — who is it — where are you?' but I received no reply.

I was exasperated and losing all comprehension of what was going on when I was greeted by an even more bewildering sight... I could not quite see the house through the thickness of the fog but I could see that every window was lit up from inside, and the music I had heard fade in and then fade out seemed to be coming from within. As I crept closer to the house, I noticed that the door was open, too, and that the hallway light was also turned on.

'Hello?' I asked again as I stepped into the house.

W.S. Barton

It was much brighter than it had been when I had been there, with all the lights on. The music was playing quite loudly and coming from upstairs. I had considered myself old enough not to be afraid of the dark and that presence of mind had been sorely tested enough — Tŷ Glo had provided a lesson in how to be scared at all times.

I ascended the staircase with care, wondering what I might ought to find. The man? The woman? I squinted my eyes when I thought of this. Could I see that mist, the haze? What about the boy whose voice I had heard but whose face, whose body in fact, I was yet to see? As I got to the top of the stairs I stopped to determine where the music was coming from, and I was able to tell that it was from the main bedroom, not because of the sound of the music, but because I suddenly heard a loud and repetitive and, most of all, suddenly frantic, BANG BANG BANG BANG, knocking, as if it were coming from the inside of the door.

It continued again, BANG BANG BANG BANG.

I had a thought of wanting to flee again but I thought to myself that I must confront whatever — whoever — it was which was creating such a disturbance.

The door was ajar as I approached it slowly, with the music blaring loud, and the BANG BANG BANG BANG continuing.

I opened the door with a jolt and shouted, 'WHO'S THERE?!' — at the same time, there was an almighty crash and bang.

The door swung back to reveal Clara, stood on a stepladder, with a hammer, obviously attempting to knock a nail in the wall, to hang a picture on. She was completely startled by my mood and frustration, as startled as I was by her presence. The frame of the picture — a painting of the lake by Waterlow Park, where we had spent many an afternoon or evening walk — had quite clearly become damaged in being dropped by Clara as a result of my surprise entrance.

She looked at me and for a few moments we said no words. The music continued to play loudly and I was able to tell it was, obviously, our record player from home. Clara climbed down off the ladder and came up to me, holding me by my shoulders.

'Well, hello to you too,' she said. 'What on earth has got into you?'

'Sorry, I...' I could barely bring myself to speak before somehow dragging myself to the bed to sit down. Clara turned the music down low.

'Finn, are you okay?'

'When did you... Sorry...'

'I came up today. I got everything sorted yesterday and I wanted to surprise you,' she said. 'Looks like we both got a bit of a surprise!'

I was sure she could tell I was deeply unsettled.

'Finn, what is wrong? Please tell me? Why did you just shout?'

'I thought that... I thought that someone had broken in,' I eventually brought myself to say.

'Why? What would make you think that?'

'The lights... the fog. The child. I don't know. How did you get here? Did you hear... is there a boy here?'

'No?!' she laughed. 'I came by car... although it was not a very pleasant drive through this fog. That hill is a nightmare! Very slowly, I got here.'

'Were you accompanied? I'm sure I heard...'

'Honestly, Finn, what has got into you?' she repeated.

'I don't know... it's so good to see you,' I hugged her tightly and for a second I wondered if I would ever let her go, until she pulled away to look at me. She was not convinced by my demeanour and did appear to be quite worried so I wondered what state I was in. I knew it could not have been great. I was not yet ready, having been completely surprised by her arrival, to tell her of the things I had experienced.

'So... what have you made of the house? How much have you seen?' I tried to make light conversation.

'Oh it's marvellous. It's so marvellous, Finn. I love it. Well, the inside anyway. Please tell me it's everything I hope it is on a clearer day, have you seen it clearer?'

'Yes... yes it is majestic when it is clear. Even when it isn't,' I replied, and I admit that I was trying to convince myself more than her.

'I can't wait to see it... so... what have you actually done?' Clara laughed at me.

'Is everything alright?' I replied, unintentionally changing the conversation, 'Everything here, you have been alright?'

'Yes, really, I love it. It's even better than I imagined... A boy, really...' she trailed off. 'Really, darling.'

I stayed sat on the bed while Clara got back up to potter around the room. She gave up on putting the painting up on account of the damaged frame but talked of the things she was going to do to the room, to the house. It was a strange atmosphere as I had returned with every intention of gathering up my belongings and going but here was my wife, in her full stride of excitement and motivation, just as I had been but a few days before. I was in two minds — as I had actually become quite accustomed to anyway — but I could not bring myself to dampen that enthusiasm and scare her unnecessarily.

I stole myself away from the bedroom and went downstairs to pour myself a drink. I did not wish to bother Clara with my concerns, hoping that the presence of someone I was familiar with would render these unusual disturbances as nothing other than the strange events that some experience with a new home. I did not want to burden her with what I had just seen, with the young teenager's death, just yet. I could discuss with her the woman, and the theories that circled around her existence, at another time.

After giving the matter some thought I admit for a few moments I did even consider that even if all the stories and tales were true; if the man was a ghost, if the ghost I had seen in my nightmare was that of Iris Argall, then what had happened in the last God-knows-how-many years?

Apparently, nothing.

Was I heartless to think that even if this tragic event that I had been witness to was in anyway connected to the supposed ghost of Iris Argall, or the vengeance of the man who had lived here, that was then indeed the sacrifice, the cost, and now it had happened, we might live in peace? And if so, what was the purpose in unnecessarily frightening Clara? There was none, she would find out soon enough, but it seemed more heartless to do that tonight. I would do whatever I could to preserve Clara's excitement about the house and the future. I could not, I did not, want to stop that this evening.

If this sounds like I was attempting to provide some kind of escapism for her, then the truth is, I was doing it for myself.

And I could not have been more relieved to have her back with me.

The mere idea of safety in numbers felt like enough to satisfy me and even the realisation that it was my wife protecting me from that feeling rather than the other way around was not enough to make me feel ashamed.

I sat with my drink whilst harbouring these thoughts, mindless of the time. Clara continued upstairs and the pitter-patter of feet and activity was wonderful. I wondered if, stood in front of the house, that movement of feet had echoed outside. An old house like this had its noises which I imagined would only serve to have made me more paranoid if I had been alone. Those innocuous and harmless bumps in the night seem like just that when you have company and I had started to notice in myself a growing tendency to perhaps give more credence to these silly things, such had been my uncertainty.

Remembering how Lillian had taught me the previous evening, I got the oven working and fired up. I was hardly likely to test my culinary skills now but felt that I ought to do everything I could to make Clara's life easier. I looked outside the kitchen window over the back of the house. My eyes went from left to right, scanning the remains of the chapel and the graveyard, to the desolate wasteland that made up the remainder of the island, to the outhouse, where I noticed that Clara had parked the car. Everything was how it should be.

Chapter Twelve
The Box

CLARA MUST have been disturbed by my starting of the oven as I noticed the slowing of the rhythm of her pottering around and she came downstairs shortly after.

'Oh,' she said, in that way that made it difficult to tell if she was genuinely surprised that I had done something I thought was helpful, or disappointed that I seemingly expected her to cook.

She quickly confirmed it was the latter.

'I thought we might go and see what there is to eat in the village or go and see Hector and Lillian.'

I pondered this for a few moments. Any trip into the village was almost certain to provoke questions from somebody, not least Clara, who may wonder why I hadn't felt it necessary to mention what I had witnessed. Of course, I had a logical explanation which my wife would be sure to understand but I still felt it too soon for that. The consequence of opening that can of worms would be discussing things that Clara might initially find difficult to rationalize and I would not expect her to because I, myself had not done so.

'I'm sure you are tired,' I suggested.

'I'm quite fine, in fact I have a bit of a spring in my step,' she replied.

'Well... I am tired myself. And I am a little uncertain about going up and down that hill in the dark,' I tried.

'Really?'

'Well, suppose we go out and there's fog, or clouds, on the way back.' I noted that Clara appeared a little unconvinced. 'I could telephone Hector and ask if they would like to come over. I can tell you that Lillian is a wonderful cook. They came over last night.'

'No... we can't ask them to come all this way if they came out last night,' Clara reluctantly acceded. 'What is there to eat?'

Lillian had brought over some meat which she had put in the huge freezer box so I went over and pulled out a joint of lamb.

'Well, we have this and some potatoes and vegetables.'

'It's huge!'

'Well, we'll have some left over for lunch tomorrow.'

'No, it will take hours to defrost,' she said with a withering glare. 'We'll have to go to the village.'

I found myself more panicked than I felt cause to be, trying to quickly think of an alternative.

'We have enough for a salad?' I meekly suggested. Surprisingly, Clara seemed to think this was a good enough idea, at least, that's what the raise of her eyebrows suggested. I continued 'You always said we should eat a little healthier and you know, we are in the country.'

'Yes... ok... I guess that wouldn't take too long,' she said.

With that, she tended to the vegetables, to a sigh of relief from myself.

In that moment of relief I considered what had made me that way for I was far more agitated than I should have been, and persistent in my requirement that we stay in the house. That in itself had surprised me. I had gone full circle since walking into the house, afraid of it and now almost afraid to leave.

No, not afraid. Reluctant.

Now that the house was filled with another character, with conversation, I was quite happy. It was as if I had been waiting for that feeling and now that it was there I didn't want to let it go. I don't know, but it felt like something more than a feeling, almost like a gravitational pull, as if I had some sort of obligation to ensure that there was a happy chatter echoing within the walls.

'I'm so glad you like the house,' I said.

'Like I said, I love it,' Clara repeated. 'I know it needs a little work doing...'

'Does it? I was afraid to touch anything... I'm afraid that's why there hasn't been much done, I mean... it's so beautiful. I never would have thought that we would be able to live in a house like this.'

'I know!' Clara agreed with more excitement in her voice. 'It's probably for the best that you didn't. We can have a look tomorrow about what we need to do. There's no rush. I just want to make it feel like our place first of all and get some familiar things around. I have the television in the lounge although I'm not quite sure whether it will stay there.'

'Really?!' I asked with more enthusiasm than was necessary, 'That is wonderful. Although there is more than enough to keep us busy... and you're right. We spent a good time in there last night and it really does feel like a room designed to hold conversation. There is a smaller lounge, a sitting room, at the front of the house.'

'Yes I know, I have done my own exploring, you know!'

Shortly, dinner was prepared and Clara and I enjoyed more positive conversation about the house. It made me think of the possibilities. For a while I had almost completely forgotten the man, the woman, the boy whose voice I was sure I had heard, the house noises, and dismissed them as just a temporary nonsense that was in the past. The subject matter changed from the immediate future to the long term.

'This is the kind of house I think I could see us living in for a long time... not just modernising and selling on,' I said.

'You really think we could fit in with this life, away from the City?'

'Yes I'm certain,' I insisted, 'Sure, we could sell the house and make a profit, but how likely are we to find another place like this? With all this space? It would be perfect to raise a family.'

'Finn...' Clara attempted to interject.

'I can just imagine what we could do,' I continued, conscious that I did not want Clara to object repeating her wish to not have children. I had hoped that I could convince her.

'What could we do? What do you mean? If our money is tied up here...'

'Well we could sell up down in London and invest our money up here. If there are bargains like this to be found—'

'Finn, that's hardly likely,' Clara interrupted.

'But if there are... even if there aren't... then money aside, surely there's more fulfillment to be had up here.'

'Let's see. We've got to settle in first. We don't even know anybody... which reminds me, have you seen or spoken to any of the locals, the previous owner?'

'Yes... yes as a matter of fact I saw him... yesterday,' I spoke carefully. 'In fact most of the locals are from the same family. Seems like they run everything in Dyffryn Du.'

'And are they friendly?'

'Well it's hard to tell... I suppose there is always some reticence when it comes to meeting somebody new. Somebody unfamiliar.'

'That sounds ominous... what have you done?'

'Oh nothing! I suppose that maybe I asked one or two many questions... you know. Why the house was so cheap.'

'And...?'

'You notice the trees outside.'

'Mmm, the stumps.'

'Yes, well, there you are. Not that I suppose it means a significant difference, but they took the wood and if we want warmth in the house then we have to go and buy it from them. And considering they're our local community then we shall have to use their conveniences,' I explained. 'So drip by drip they'll get money.'

'I suppose. But like you say it still doesn't explain it.'

'No,' I said. I refused to go further or hint that there may be more. 'Either that, or, we'll have to mine for coal!'

The night drew in and so we retired to the sitting room to watch the television. Again, I found it entertaining that the television, a modern invention, was placed in this most ancient of settings. The big unit appeared ugly and obscene amongst this most wonderfully presented house but at least we were able to indulge in some escapism before deciding to call it a night and go to bed. We talked, but when we did, it was about nothing in particular. It was comfortable.

We had been in bed for a short time — deciding to go straight to sleep rather than read or talk for a bit. It had been a long day and the events of it continued to whirl around my head. I ought to have been exhausted but now, with no noise, nothing else to concentrate on but my own thoughts, I couldn't put the image of the young girl, lifeless on the floor, out of my head. I had tried so stubbornly to push it out of my mind but I knew that at some point I must internally process the trauma. Suppressing such an event would only cause its manifestation elsewhere. It was very disturbing as I invited the thoughts in against natural resistance. That in itself must have exhausted me. I must have fallen asleep because the next thing I remembered was Clara gently waking me.

'Darling... Finn... Finn,' she said softly.

I stirred. It was still dark.

'I heard a noise outside. It sounds like there are people outside,' she said once she knew I was awake. 'Will you go and check?'

'It's probably just the kids,' I said.

'What kids?'

Of course, I hadn't mentioned the teenagers. When I came around I wondered why they would be here. I had seen one of them, Lauren, die just hours earlier. I was able to rouse myself and get out of bed.

'Don't worry, I'll check.'

I walked out of the bedroom and in to the smaller bedroom overlooking the back. As I approached it I could already hear the sound of voices out of the back and sure enough, there were bodies in the distance moving around. I was unable to make out their faces but there were three of them and it was a natural assumption I came to that it must have been the boys and Macy, the other girl, from the other night. I turned on the light of the room and thought it may give me a bit of a better look outside and I was able to determine that my assumption was correct. The light disturbed them so one of the boys walked towards the house, close enough for me to see him, and waved up at me. I waved back down and motioned with my hand to keep the noise down. He gave the thumbs up and moved back to his friends.

I thought it best to leave them as they were obviously grieving and perhaps this was the best way for them. They had been respectful the other night and I had no appetite to create any conflict tonight.

Instead, I turned off the light and returned to the bedroom.

'Clara it's just some teenagers. They were here the other night,' I said, cautious of revealing further details. It wasn't a conversation for this moment in time. 'They're quite harmless. They camp out on the field.'

'They were loud, I don't want them shouting and running about. We need to sleep.'

'Yes of course, don't worry, they know to keep down the noise.'

'Are you sure? If it carries on, will you go out?'

'Yes, yes, I promise, now let's go back to sleep,' I said, getting back into bed and turning off the lamp.

I must have fallen to sleep quite quickly as I don't remember being unduly troubled by any further thoughts; that was until I was woken again, by Clara again.

'Finn, they're still making noise,' she said.

After a few seconds composing myself I tried to listen for sounds outside. I could hear nothing but a howling wind which had picked up.

'Clara it's quiet. It's just the wind,' I said. I looked at my watch. 'And it's 2:20am. They're probably asleep just like we should be.'

'I heard them,' she insisted. 'Please just go and say something.'

I reluctantly rose and made my way to the staircase. The darkness of the landing made it difficult to see too far in front of myself for it was mostly black, broken by the moonlight shining through the window and providing some visible guidelines via the stairs.

As I turned the corner I could have sworn that the haze which I had seen the other morning, the smog from which the woman had materialised in my nightmare, was lingering up on our upper level, bringing with it a cold that swept over my arms, gently spraying them with water. I looked at my arms and sure enough, I could see the light of my arm hairs wet at the tips as if they were individual grass stems covered in the morning dew. Surely just a trick of the mind? I wiped my eyes and I looked closely about myself but couldn't see anything so I made my way to, and then down, the stairs, moving to the kitchen and out through the back door.

I walked towards the chapel but could instantly tell that there was nobody there. The wind was bitter and swift, so strong that I had to carefully watch my step.

There was no tent, no sign that they had even been there. They must have decided to leave once they saw that I had been disturbed enough to wake up. Or they must have been put off by the wind. I turned back and made my way to the house.

I locked the kitchen door and turned around to leave the room when I noticed something on the table, reflecting in the light.

It was the small silver box.

I walked towards the table and looked around. Clara was not downstairs as she would have certainly have turned the lights on and probably followed me into the kitchen. She could not have brought the box and placed it on to the table and it most certainly wasn't there when we finished our dinner.

I touched the box and went to lift the lid. To my surprise it opened quite easily to reveal a red velvet cloth. I peeled the cloth back and, exactly like the contents of my dream, or nightmare, sat some toy soldiers and farmyard animals and a small train made out of tin. But how? How could that be so? I had not seen the box open, much less knew of its contents; save for my own imagination from my nightmare.

I was sure I was awake now and I was at a loss to explain the presence of the box and its contents. Could it have been a trick from the teenagers? How would they have got in? Why would they want to do this — and how would they even know the significance? No, there was a reason, but it was a reason I was not prepared to accept. I looked further, pulling the soldiers, animals and the train out, discarding the cloth, and found a small, folded piece of paper. I opened it carefully and saw a drawing, a drawing of a man fishing by a stream in front of a house — this house — with a boy and mother stood in the doorway, watching on. It was signed Jack Howell, six.

I felt the hairs on my body begin to stand on end, as if in anticipation of a cold wave they had noticed before my brain had managed to calculate what was happening. I suddenly felt that same feeling of being closed in, surrounded even, but when I looked around, I could see I was alone.

I looked around again before moving swiftly to the bedroom. As I prepared to scale the stairs I shouted 'Clara!' and she responded to ask me what was wrong. I realised I must have sounded a little panicked but I was anxious to hear the sound of something real, something tangible, something that wasn't a trick of the imagination, a trick of the light.

I got into the bedroom.

'What is it, what's wrong?'

I struggled to find the words.

'Have they done something to you?'

'No... there's no-one there.'

'Really?'

With this, as if disbelieving me, Clara rose out of bed and looked out of the front window over the land and towards the start of The Snake's decent. As far as I could tell, she could see nobody, or nothing, and if she did she didn't mention it.

'Honestly, I swear I heard them,' she said.

'You may well have, they might have been leaving... but

there's no-one there now.'

She looked at me, unconvinced.

'I went outside and checked,' I said.

'Yes I know, I heard the door go... I don't know. Maybe it was the wind.'

'Anyway... did you come downstairs at all?' I asked.

'No, why?'

There was no way I could attempt to explain the silver box, not at this present time, but I concluded that I would share all at breakfast. I couldn't tolerate living with having all of what I was going through held within my mind. Before long, Clara would think I was going mad.

'Oh, I just thought I heard you when I came back in,' I lied. 'That's why I shouted before I came up.'

'Hopefully now we'll be able to get some sleep,' she said.

She certainly did, but I was unable.

The wind continued to swirl and consequently there were all manners of knocks and unfamiliar creaks and noises through the house that made my mind wander.

It was still dark outside when I finally decided to give up on the opportunity of getting any sleep and go downstairs. The merest hint of dawn was enough to convince me that I was not going to get any proper sleep and so I made my way down into the kitchen to make myself a glass of water. On the table remained the box, just how I'd left it, open with its contents showing. I sat down at the table, looking at the soldiers, looking at the toy train, the piece of paper that I had folded back up.

Of course, in the dead of night, these inanimate objects had appeared quite sinister merely by virtue of their existence yet now, with morning breaking, they appeared just as they are.

Effectively harmless, meaningless little trinkets. I imagined the most danger one might suffer from one of them is swallowing them by accident or perhaps the discomfort of stepping on one. Foolish, really, though I was still quite concerned by the fact I had foreshadowed the contents of the box. I became curious about my own condition. Was I going mad? I was of sober and sound enough mind at this moment. I didn't feel particularly special, psychologically connected to anything.

After a little while of coming around I made my way into the library. I sat at the desk and harmlessly swung my legs as I got comfortable, feeling a little restless. I stood up and looked through the books again and noticed that one had no title at all and so I picked it out and went and sat back down.

I opened it and realised it must have been a record, a diary of some sort. There were individual papers between the pages. I flicked through and noted that it was nothing other than a planner, but with nothing of note in there aside from dates of birthdays, of names I had no cause to recognise, and such. Stuck to one of the pages was what appeared to be a dusty family photograph. I wiped it with the sleeve of my shirt and looked at it.

A mother and father and a child, sat outside, and if I wasn't mistaken, it was outside this very house. I smiled — the man looked a little like me, I thought. In fact, he bore more than a passing resemblance, even I could see that. How strange. I thought more — given the fact that this house had been abandoned for so long, these people were surely to be Iris Argall, her husband and their youngest boy. It may well have been their eldest before their youngest came along. Amused by how the man looked like me, I took the picture to one side out of the book and my curiosity led me to check my own birthday, in February. It was strange, but I almost had expected to see something written there, my own name even, and was a little disappointed when I saw that it wasn't.

I continued to read the book and saw that, aside from the family portrait, the diary was empty — the other individual papers were in fact meaningless advertisements, ripped from the local newspaper, and I took to looking at them, to see if there was some reason they may have been kept, separated and preserved, but there apparently was none.

I sat back, frustrated, wondering if I ought to go outside. I was quite restless. But, my curiosity had not taken me to good places since I had arrived in Tŷ Glo and I had no particular rush to suffer any more frights. I sat for some time until I heard some noise from upstairs, suggesting that Clara was getting up for the day. Soothed by the reassurance of movement, company, I sat back in the chair, and must have begun to drift off. I was so exhausted.

Initially it was hard to make out anything at all. The sound was scratchy, muffled and unclear. It was only after a short while that I was able to reasonably assume that it was coming from outside, voices that came in and out of audible range. I could tell that there were quickened footsteps of a child running around and playing but it was difficult to make out any more notable sounds. I was so tired that I could barely concentrate.

'Come now, come now,' spoke a woman, clearly speaking to the child and asking them to stop playing. 'Come now,' she snapped, now panicked, and a little harsher when she was clearly not being obeyed.

'But Mummy'... said a familiar voice. I couldn't quite work it out until it became very obvious.

'Daddy! Daddy!' called the child, a young boy, unmistakably the same voice I had heard on these grounds.

Then shuffling. An emergence. A panic in the scratching.

Then, a frantic, BANG, BANG, BANG, BANG, this time, as if it were on a window, the window right behind me.

'Finn! Finn! Come here!' Clara yelled from upstairs.

It startled me out of my daydream.

I raced up the stairs, while Clara called my name again, and so I was able to tell she was in the room I had assumed was a work space.

To say I was stunned when I opened the door was an understatement. My sole foray into this room previously had found it exactly as you might have expected to, in keeping with the rest of the house, but now, to my genuine amazement, it seemed dustier, as if it had been locked for years and years. The mannequins were covered with dust; I reasoned it was simply impossible to have accumulated so heavily in the space of a day. I looked at Clara stunned but she was taken by something else with her hand over her mouth, stood by the window.

'What is it? Did you...?' I begun to ask, walking over to her. As I reached her, she pulled her finger up, and it was trembling furiously as she pointed it outside.

I looked out over the back of the house and could not quite make out what had moved Clara into such a state until I gazed past the chapel and the graveyard and my eyes were drawn to the shape of what was indisputably a human body, face down in the water, close to the edge of the field.

I reeled — suddenly the state of the room was of little consequence as I raced down the stairs and out of the house so fast that it felt for a second as if I were flying. I ran out of the kitchen door, to the chapel, past the graveyard to the edge of the water where I waded in and dragged the body to dry ground. It was that of a girl — when I turned the body around to see the face I could quite clearly see, though the face was drained and blue, that it was that of Macy, James Appleton's other daughter and the other girl who I had seen here over two separate nights. I held her and looked at her for a few seconds before I realised there was nothing I, or anybody, could do to save her. She was gone.

Chapter Thirteen
Back in Aberaernavon

THE NEXT three hours were nothing but an awful blur. First, the Appleton's arrived, then an ambulance, then the police, and then Hector. It took a considerably long time to control myself from shaking and I was in no state to console Clara or offer any kind of explanation to James or his wife. I had none, or none that any of us wanted to speak of. Even if I had some belief or knowledge of what had happened or why, I was unable to speak of it because it was so absurd and so terribly and profoundly tragic that it would serve no purpose to share.

And, I gathered, for all it was worth, if I was right in what I was growing to accept — that the story and the 'legend' of Tŷ Glo, the man, and Iris Argall — then what comfort would anyone gain from my announcing it? The family would not have appreciated it and I would have a lot of explaining to do to Clara.

I felt utterly distraught and sick, not just because of the horror of finding and holding the body of the girl, but because it was impossible to escape any conclusion that didn't link our presence to this event. Had I unwittingly triggered it? Again? I did not need the confirmation of the doctor or paramedics to establish that she had been in the water for quite some time but I couldn't help but think that the discovery of the box in the dead of... in the middle of the night was intrinsically connected to this event.

The police said nothing of note but from the tone and nature of what they were saying they seemed keen to categorise it as anything other than a tragic accident.

I knew otherwise.

This was no accident. At one point I even overheard one of the police officers suggest that Macy had been so traumatised by the death of her sister just two days before that she may have had cause to take her own life — this, as you would expect, was not received favourably by the Appletons.

Neither Clara nor I attempted to resist Hector's determination to take us away from the house back into the village and Paul — who had arrived shortly after his brother — said we would be welcome back at the White Horse, so we made our way there for a stiff drink.

Once there I explained as much as I reasonably could to Clara about what I had experienced. The stories, tales I had heard, the death of Macy's sister, the story of the house, of Iris Argall and her children, and the man that I had seen on the grounds of Tŷ Glo. I was quite insistent, even in front of Hector who appeared somewhat reluctant to entertain the discussion of having seen her when he came over with Lillian.

'It must be true. The house has been left for so long and now it has been disturbed and people are...' I said.

'I can't listen to this,' Hector said, and he got up and went to the bar.

'Look, Finn,' said Clara, clearly of more rational mind than

I was. 'It is so tragic that two young girls have died... but they are accidents.'

'No, it's more than that,' I said. 'It's too much to dismiss as coincidence. I've tried.'

'Finn, really. You've been through a lot.'

'Well how do you explain the bedroom then?' I questioned. Clara looked puzzled.

'Did you not go in it yesterday? The room with the mannequins?'

'No...'

'I was in it. I've been in it twice. The other day and it was... there was little there other than to tell it was a work space. And well kept, as if someone had been working in it last week. And today it was as if nobody had been in there for years.'

'How can I begin to explain something that I have no knowledge of?' Clara asked, putting her hands on mine, perhaps not quite understanding how apt her words were.

'Are you sure you went in there before?'

'I feel... I feel as if this is personal.' I continued.

'Now you're being silly. If it is personal against anyone then it isn't you, is it? I'm here, I'm safe... you're here and you're safe,' she attempted to re-assure me.

'No, you don't understand. That's the thing. I feel as if I have agitated... disturbed something I shouldn't have. I can't explain. I don't really understand it myself. At the same time I feel as if there is a reason or a purpose for me or us being there, like it was meant to happen for either good or bad.'

Clara's face now expressed sincere concern. That is not to say she was particularly disbelieving of me but she had presumably and understandably just assumed that I had been traumatised by the events of the morning and was now making statements based on those events.

'Believe me,' I implored. 'Something isn't right, besides the obvious. I can't speak to anyone here because they simply pretend it isn't happening... well, they won't now I suppose... but anyway I cannot explain it all to you. Unless you had seen him, the anger in his eyes, unless you had felt the presence.'

'And these are ghosts?'

'Yes... they must be,' I said, noting Clara's suspicious glare. 'Yes, I'm sure. Unless a voice can echo around those empty walls forever more. And a boy. I keep hearing the voice of a boy, of around six years old, and... what?'

Clara's eyes widened and then sharpened.

'Nothing, I'm listening, go on.'

'The boy keeps calling for his father.'

'But how can it be?'

'I don't know... I can't explain. I am not one to believe in fairy tales and anything that is not reasonable, that which cannot be explained. The man is real, as real as you or I. I have heard these stories of the woman and her children and I don't know if it is my mind playing tricks but she comes to me in my nightmares... she just...'

'Finn, I hate to see you like this. It's not you...' Her hands tightened on mine, sympathetically. 'Let's go home.'

'No, no, I'm not ready...'

'I don't mean there. I mean home, to London. You're not right, darling. You're not yourself.'

'So you believe me?' I was relieved.

'I believe that... look, I believe everything you say,' she said, meeting my eyes with conviction, though I couldn't quite tell if she meant that she believed in what I had seen or what I thought I had seen. 'We should go for a walk at least, to get some fresh air. It might make you look at things differently or come to a different perspective.' Clara said.

She rose and held my hand but then Hector paid us attention and stopped us, saying he insisted we went back with him to Aberaernavon and he would let us stay in the room we had previously used. He appeared to be in quite a hurry to get home himself and so we accepted his offer and went back to the Percy Arms.

After arriving back in Aberaernavon Clara and I decided to go for a walk, to give Hector some time alone with Lillian. It was not a conversation I wished to take part in, having seen Lillian's propensity to be upset regarding this particular subject matter.

We walked into the hills, not quite as far as we had previously, but far enough to be quite isolated and feel that we were by ourselves. I felt that for a few minutes — which seemed much longer — we both seemed eager to break the silence but hesitant that the other was about to.

It was a strange time. Clara and I knew each other so well but now, where we were, it felt as if we had spent much longer than two days apart, as if there were things between us, things we hadn't said. And we shared everything.

'You know... I know it's so sad what happened to that girl and I do believe you, but I just think we should go back to the house. I know I said we should go to London but now I'm thinking it was just the shock talking,' said Clara.

'I don't think...' I tried, before trailing off, realising that I needn't say anymore. I just shook my head.

'We can sell the house. But let's do it the right way, we can't just run away. How would that look?'

'The police... the Appleton's... they all know... think... it was an accident.'

'But if we were to rush away hurriedly then how would that look?' she insisted.

I remained unconvinced.

'Well, what if I go there?' Clara said.

'No!' I snapped. 'You can't.'

'It could hardly be so terrible.'

'It is.'

'I don't mean to patronise you and I know that you have been through a lot, and I believe you when you tell me what you have seen, but I cannot believe that we will be scared away from a huge investment, our livelihood, because of some old tale that you have started to believe,' Clara said sternly.

I didn't know how to respond at first.

'I would have loved to stay there. I really would.' I admitted. 'As I said to you just yesterday...'

'What has changed since then?' Clara interrupted.

'You know what!'

'What more can I say? It is sad but surely her friends knew the risk in leaving her alone. Surely they all knew the risk fooling around in water in the dark.'

'But...'

'It was an accident.'

'Suppose it was? Suppose we stay at Tŷ Glo and everything goes as planned? Then what?'

'What do you mean?'

'Well you have already said that you are not willing to have children. Even if... even if everything was perfect with that place then how am I supposed to live with that?'

'Really, Finn, I don't think you're in the right frame of mind for this conversation.'

'What do you mean?' She said nothing. 'The house, the land, it is so vast that to have it so isolated and hold just you and I for years and years...'

'It wouldn't be isolated, we could run a hotel.'

'Nobody would stay there.'

'They would!'

There seemed to be no talking to her.

'You can't just make a decision like that on your own. You can't just say you don't want children.'

'Finn, I can't. I can't.'

'Can't what?'

'I can't have children, okay, are you happy?!' Clara growled at me, tears in her eyes.

'What...'

'I didn't want to say. I hoped I would never have to say.'

'You have to tell me.'

Clara stood up and walked away, agitated and anxious. I had to follow.

'You have to tell me, Clara,' I repeated.

'You will hate me. You will never want to talk to me again.'

'What is it? You're scaring me? Nothing could be quite that bad.'

She sat down again, and held my hand and my stare.

'After... after your dad died,' she began, 'I found out I was pregnant.'

'What? Why didn't you tell me?'

'I just... you were so upset.'

'Well that would have been a good thing, a pleasant distraction, surely? But what...'

'I thought you might find it selfish of me, that you might resent me...'

'What happened?' There was a sternness to my voice I barely recognised.

'I panicked. I didn't know what to do. We were both working so hard. We were barely spending any time together...'

'Clara...'

'I didn't know what to do for the best... so I had...'

She didn't need to say it.

'An abortion. An abortion. You..?'

Her sudden stream of tears was confirmation, and her grip on my hands tightened as if to stop my impulsion to move away in disgust.

'How could you? Why, why would you?' I said, unsure if I wanted an answer, before happening on a realisation of my own. 'But when? You said when my father died. That would have been illegal? Who did it?'

I wanted to be compassionate but it was hard to understand that the woman I was looking at, the woman I'd known and shared almost half my life with, was suddenly unfamiliar to me. How could she have lived with this?

'Who did it?!'

'I found a doctor.'

I struggled to comprehend how she would even have started such a process and felt too sick to ask.

'I can't listen to this,' I broke myself away from her, stood and started to walk away.

'Finn, please,' Clara said, standing up and running after me, grabbing me. 'I'm sorry, I'm sorry, I have regretted it ever since. ' 'If you regret it so much, then why, why must you continue to hurt me? Was it not mine? Were you having an affair?'

'No, of course not. I love you, I only love you,' she protested through her cries.

'Then why, if you regret it, do you insist on not having children? What did I do to deserve all this?'

'I can't, that's why. There were complications. The abortion went... it went wrong. And they said I couldn't have children. I wish I could. That's all I want to give you.'

She was barely able to complete the last sentence through fear and upset.

I did not know what to do. In that instance I saw a vulnerability and an honesty that provoked compassion. I could not hold back. I was still angry, bitterly angry, but such was my love for Clara that I was unable to bear to see her so heartbroken. I held her as tenderly as if nothing had happened and her honest and strong hold of me made me melt a little.

We stood there for some time, her crying in my arms, and me trying to compose myself.

'I'm sorry. I'm so sorry,' she whispered.

We walked back down the hills — the way we came this time, not down to the pre-fab — and back to the Percy Arms in silence. I ran Clara a bath and after she had washed and got out, I got in it myself.

Though I felt like it, I did not cry. There were so many thoughts going around my mind that I felt if I started to cry I might not stop. I couldn't help but think of when I had tried to bring the topic up before and how Clara's response to me feeling things were fated was so bleak.

'As far as I can tell, only two things are. Life... and death. All in between is a matter of happenchance,' she had said to me.

I attempted, as best I could, to push all upsetting thoughts out of my mind and relax. It worked for a while but after but a few moments of tranquility a horrid feeling crept over the hairs of my neck, a pure moment of dread, almost as if I were suffering some awful premonition.

In that few seconds all I could think about was the man on the land and how he had looked at me at the back of the house. It was an unwelcome thought but I could not move it from my mind. My perception of that glare had changed from it being simply unwelcoming to now, vengeful. I could picture it vividly in my mind and it caused me to feel goosebumps all over my arms. I tried to shut that out of my mind and at once I could see the woman from my visions, who I was sure was Iris Argall, now, as clearly as I saw the man. Her expression was one of anguish, desperate fear, now almost pleading with me to help, and at once, I opened my eyes to try and rid myself of the image.

I jolted myself out of the thought and jumped with some emergency out of the bath, immediately desperate to go to Clara just so that I would have some company.

But Clara was not in the bedroom. I called out, though pointless, and looked out of the room door into the corridor, but couldn't see anything. I looked out of the window but could not see her. Quickly, I dressed, not bothering to properly dry myself, and went down into the lounge. There was Hector, by himself, at the bar with a few locals in.

'Have you seen Clara?' I asked.

'No... I thought you had gone to your room?'

'Is she with Lillian?'

'No, she'd have to come through here. I've been here since you came back.'

A panic came over me — where could she be? I walked out into the street and, while it was early evening, with the sun setting, I was able to tell that she wasn't there. It didn't stop me shouting out. I did not want to think the obvious but I had no choice and so after going back to check the room — though where I might have expected her to pop up from was against all rational thought — I asked Hector if he would mind taking me to Tŷ Glo.

The colour ran from his face.

'Why do you want to go back, son? Why?' he asked.

'Clara's gone there. She must have.'

'She knows better than that, surely.'

'She... she thinks it's just fantasy.'

'I... Son, come through.'

With that, Hector opened up the bar for me to walk through to the back.

'I can't go there. I can't go back,' he said to me quietly.

'But why? You've been there a few times now' I said. 'And you have seen her. You have seen Iris Argall too. And...'

'No,' he cut me off sharp, harsh, to keep my voice down, 'that could have been the light.' Neither of us were convinced. 'I did not see her,' he insisted. 'I do not want to live with that young girl's life on my conscience. And you should not too. I hope you know that this comes from a good place but you should not stay here. I... I can't have it around Lillian.'

'Tell me, tell me why it so deeply affects her,' I asked.

'Her sister was... before Lillian was born, her parents had another little girl, who died young. They moved out of Dyffryn Du and they always said Lillian was a blessing,' said Hector. 'The other night... she has been haunted by this her entire life. She doesn't need this. You understand that I can't go back with you.' It was delivered as more of a statement than a question.

'Yes... yes of course. But I must. Clara is there and I must go.'

'You can take my car, but please, come straight back,' he asked, with a look of genuine concern.

'Yes, thank you, of course.'

Hector duly gave me his keys and walked me out to the car. He gave me a hug, and then I got in the motor and commenced my drive back to get Clara.

CHAPTER FOURTEEN
Rescue

MY MIND was racing, full of a million different thoughts as I drove. For one so prone to procrastination the last few days had proved excruciating and on one occasion, close to where the area Lauren had been killed in the car accident, I had to stop and regulate my breathing such was my anxiety.

In that paused moment I felt both clarity and confusion, simultaneously drawn and repulsed by the idea of going to the house. I tried to comprehend why Clara felt the need to go back and all I could really conclude was that she wanted to make it easier for me, that she would be packing our belongings and returning. In that event she was far less likely to be as fearful and anxious as I was so I felt it would be better if I composed myself so as not to arrive looking as delirious as I felt.

I started to drive and almost wanted to close my eyes as I passed where Lauren had been knocked over — a spot now decorated by a small bunch of flowers and a bear — which, upon seeing, became very difficult indeed. Nonetheless I continued my journey, passing the White Horse which appeared closed but had lights on. My guess was that the family was continuing to grieve in private, but then, owning much of the village as they did, that was understandable.

I drove until I got to the start of 'The Snake' and realised that my hands were shaking. I had to compose myself as I was driving too fast to be considered anything other than reckless and I was not familiar enough with the hill as yet to be driving up it on a day with as poor visibility as today.

I briefly turned the radio on but turned it off as the signal was sketchy. I was just hopeful of anything to distract me from my own thoughts but out here, as far as I had driven, and still impossibly far from where I needed to be, I felt in some sort of pained limbo, agitated and impatient to get to my wife and also unnerved by the eerie atmosphere which surrounded me. These villages had provided quite an unusual atmosphere anyway. With the events of today, as understandable as it was, that inclusive, separated feeling was tangible. I was isolated and I felt that way practically and metaphorically.

Unable to do anything but dwell on my own thoughts I wondered what might await me in the house. The box, the man? Oh God, I thought. What if Clara had seen the man, and been unable to move away, to travel back down? What if she was trapped there? I remembered at once my own feeling of dread which had stayed with me as clear as the second it came on, and worried that Clara may possibly have been faced with the same sort of predicament.

Then, again, my thoughts of Clara made me ponder why she had gone back. I was still reeling from her revelation but she had seemed quite apologetic and remorseful. I was hurt — I did not yet understand her reasons. But I was still in love with her, and willing to listen to why she had done what she had. I did not want to think of the long term future beyond leaving

Dyffryn Du and going back to London. Learning more of the consequences of her actions could wait for another time.

I thought of how long she had had to dwell on this, to regret it and carry it around with her. It must have been almost seven years since my father passed away. That would have made our child six years old, already educated to some extent, with their own character, the perfect age at which to romp around the grounds we had just acquired.

Just at the moment my restlessness and anxiety began to overcome me, I stopped myself and just held tightly on to the wheel. I felt a momentary wave of calm. I supposed it was still risky but in my irrational state of mind I did not want to wait, I just wanted to get to Clara.

I still drove at some speed, braking harshly as I reached the top of the hill, and I jumped out of the car. I stared at the house. It looked dark, un-entered. I searched my pockets and then realised that Clara must have the keys.

I walked up the pathway, listening carefully for any sound, but I heard nothing but wind. It was not quite as violent as it had been last night but still strong enough to bring a chill. Up as high as I was, I reckoned that if the ferocity of the wind was any greater, it would unsettle me greatly.

The door was locked.

'Clara!' I knocked and yelled. 'It's me, let me in!'

I knocked again after receiving no response.

Perhaps she was upstairs, she couldn't hear me. I listened at the door but could hear nothing — it was so thick, though, that I couldn't have expected to. If she couldn't hear me knocking, though, then that was another thing altogether.

I quickly made my away around the side of the house. This

time I chose to go around my right hand side, avoiding the chapel and the gravestones, for I did not want to approach the area where we had found the young girl earlier in the day. Approaching the back, I noticed that our car was still there, and when I got to the kitchen door, I was a little relieved to find it open.

I entered the house through the kitchen, once again acknowledging the silver tin on the table.

'Hello?' I said loudly, hoping to hear a response. 'Clara... Clara, are you there?'

I received no reply but noticed as I got to the kitchen door that I could hear the sound of the television coming from the lounge. Not the sound of a television show, or the news, but that gentle static hum that vividly let you know that the television was on. I walked there quite briskly, fully expecting Clara to be sat inside, but as I opened the door, it was empty, save of course for its contents and the television which was playing, with its static and snow.

I stood at the doorway and shouted her name again but once more received no reply. Confused, concerned, I tentatively walked inside the room, when the television suddenly flickered, spluttered and went off. I flicked the light switch — it didn't come on. Power cut.

At once, once more, my body seemed to react quicker than my mind, suffering that heightened tension and anxiety. Against the dark I could see a deviation in front of me, as if my eyes were playing a trick. I knew instantly it must have been the same gas fume-style visual obstruction I had fell victim to before, but now, it was real, in front of my eyes, surrounding me.

Then 'Daddy!' — the voice of the young boy filled the

hallway, startling me to turn around. There was no mistaking it, the same voice I had heard. A boy of what, six? Six years old... surely it was too much of a painful coincidence to think that the voices I had been hearing in the house could have been that of my own boy? No, no... that would be absurd, too much to take.

'Daddy!'

Now a little quieter.

The voice was coming from the library.

I walked, cautiously, to the room, opening the door.

'Daddy... Daddy... Daddy...'

Nothing. I didn't know whether to feel relieved or afraid, but I do know my state of anxiety was beginning to grow. I looked around me but could see nothing, and I carefully narrowed my eyes to try and see the smoggy obstruction but all seemed fine.

The silence revealed another sound. The shuffling of furniture from upstairs, as if somebody was moving a table, or at least, heavy objects.

'Clara?' I shouted from the hallway.

More shuffling and then, nothing. It was a sound I was able to recognise, identical to the scratching I had heard coming from there the other night, but now, clearly, I was able to tell that it was furniture. I walked to the bottom of the staircase and waited to hear another sound for a few moments but could not hear any movement whatsoever. This house could amplify the quietest noise but when it was silent it carried a surreal atmosphere.

'Clara?'

THUD.

The sound of furniture being moved or thrown on to the floor came distinctly from the room with the mannequins.

BANG BANG BANG BANG BANG.

It was a frantic, desperate sound, banging against the door.

BANG BANG BANG BANG.

This time, as if it were against the bedroom window, as if the person banging was trying to smash it or get out of it.

Then, the most sickening and horrendous wail I had ever heard in my life, a haunted screech that caused me to wince in the same way that one does when hearing squeaky chalk scratch on a board.

I ran upstairs powered by adrenalin and momentum but when I reached the top and realised that all the lights were still off, I was decidedly more hesitant to approach the room.

'Clara?' I said again, realising the pointlessness at this stage, but wanting to signal a loud enough warning to whomever — whatever — was here if Clara was not answering.

As I reached the bedroom I slowly twisted the handle and pushed it forward to reveal a small cabinet had been obstructing its opening. I pushed harder, to reveal the inside of the room, and with a show of strength I didn't know I had within myself, I knocked the cabinet over and the door swung open.

I could barely believe my eyes.

The mannequins decorated the room, making it difficult for me to understand what I was seeing. For a moment, I felt as if the room was populated by a number of real people, a feeling that intensified when I suddenly noticed movement.

There, banging on the window was the very clear shape

of the woman I had seen formed by the mist, the woman I took to be Iris Argall. With one hand, she appeared to be banging against the glass, but I could now hear no sound, and with the other, she protected a young child.

'Iris...' I said.

As if I was compelled against my will I somehow found myself move closer to them. I am not able to describe this action — something like an impulsive human nature to react and save somebody, even though I knew that these were beings that could not be saved, even their souls were long gone. But move forward I did.

As I moved forward, the bodies in front of me began to become engulfed with flames, the banging against the panes still silent. Their growing illumination against the shadowed silhouettes of the mannequins was eerie beyond words.

'Iris!' I shouted, now.

The figure turned to me and it was horrendous. The flames evaporated. Her eyes opened, immediately fixed on mine, as if there was nothing wrong with her, and I had been lured here. There, closer than I had ever been to this figure, and as real as I'd ever seen her, I was able to see the most pure of hatred and animosity spewing from her eyes and for a second, I almost felt as if she was smiling, or grimacing, at me. My eyes moved from hers only to examine her face which I now realised was suffering from horrific burns, so traumatic that I would have thought it incomprehensible that she was still alive, if I had not realised that she was not. I could not bring myself to look at the child. She seemed to move towards me and for a moment, the silhouette of her figure seemed to blend in with that of the mannequins, with only her face visible.

It was only a few seconds — two, three — but it felt like an eternity. My neck suffered a spasm which shocked me and once my eyes were disconnected from hers I was able to scramble out of the door, refusing to look back and almost on my knees I crawled and managed my way to the stairs.

Held up by the bannister, I pushed my way down the stair-case, and my journey was punctuated by the returned static sound of the television from the lounge and then the repeated voice of the child.

'Daddy... Daddy... Daddy...'

I tried to cover my ears but it couldn't stop the sound.

'Shut up, stop it, STOP IT!' I shouted out in panic, somehow finding the energy to move myself down the stairs and towards the kitchen. As I did, I noticed that there was a child, a boy, sat with his back to me at the table, playing with the toy soldiers from the box.

'Daddy, come here, look,' said the boy, innocently, still with his back to me.

I turned and fled for the front door, terrified out of my skin. I tried to open it but it was locked and so I banged and I banged on it. I felt as if my body was contorting, pushing itself, almost trying to somehow go through the door as if I myself were a ghost. I was unable to budge the door one little bit and so I ran to the library, hoping that maybe I could use something to smash one of the windows and climb through.

I picked up a chair and tried to throw it at the window but my attempt was feeble and weak; I had become so drained that I did not seem to be able to muster the energy. It was only then that I noticed I was crying uncontrollably, and I folded to the floor in a heap, sat in the corner, almost hiding behind the chair.

Eventually I stopped sobbing and noted that it was quiet. And all was still, but I was much too frightened to move to check. All I could hear was the sound of my own heavy breathing, and that was a struggle to control for some time. I was anxious to find and rescue Clara but I am ashamed to admit that I could not move out of fear. I do not know how long I was cowered in that corner but it must have been a few hours because it felt like days.

I sat, still, and there was still no sound, not even wind, not even a creak of the house. Then, a familiar sound, the scuffle of furniture on the floor. Then silence. I closed my eyes and waited. And then came the hard repeated thud of what I now knew to be banging on the door, banging on the window, a desperation to escape, followed by the stomach-turning, nauseating cry of the burning woman unable to save her or her child.

'It's not happening, it's not happening,' I tried to tell myself, putting my hands over my ears, for a good few seconds, until the howl had stopped. All remained quiet.

After some time I summoned the power and will to pull myself up and look out of the window. I contemplated walking back into the house but I got the better of the bravery within me and was able to brush that off as sheer foolishness. No, I would summon the strength to lift the chair and smash it through the window.

I stood firmly and composed myself, waiting until I was strong enough to stand rigidly and grab the chair rather than use it as a support. At that moment I looked back outside and made out something coming towards the house. I squinted my eyes. Hector? Clara?

No, as it came closer, I noticed it was the man, the man I

had seen fishing, who had seemed to warn me away with his glare. He approached the house and then stood. He surveyed the upper windows and then walked a little more. He stood again, and this time, looked at the windows of the room I was inside. He looked right at me, and smiled. Then, he walked around the side of the house, out of view, and I heard the repeated banging of the door, the repeated banging on the window, the screams of the boy shouting for his father, and the wails of the mother unable to save her child.

Part of me wanted to race out, race upstairs. But another part of me knew and understood that there was no way I could. Nobody could. I could not put myself through that again.

For a long time afterwards there was nothing but silence and I eventually plucked up the courage to go back in to the house and think about leaving through the kitchen. As I stood in the doorway of the library every hair on my body shot on end as I heard it again — the scrape of the furniture pulling back along the floor... the pregnant silence which followed. The silence. The sound of the banging. The shriek and squeal of Iris Argall which dissipated as she and her child lost their battles. The silence which followed, which I took to be an invitation from Iris to revel and wallow in the same misery. Perhaps even suffer the same fate. It was an invitation I would not accept. But I was trapped on my own. I could not leave.

I admit to having grown delirious in my confinement. Terrified of possibly hearing the horrendous noises from above and from not being confident enough to look out of the window lest I saw something as absurdly frightening as

I had. I noted, though, that the bottle of brandy Hector had brought over was on the desk, and so I shuffled over on the floor and reached up to get it. I drunk from the bottle and the first few drinks did nothing, so I kept on, until I felt numbed. Eventually I had drunk enough to make me confident enough to stand strong and walk swiftly to the doorway. I held the doorframe, expecting the worst and bracing myself for it.

Nothing.

I walked into the hallway and everything was still quiet. I peered into the kitchen and it seemed empty — I walked there briskly and it was just that. In fact, even the silver box had disappeared.

I listened carefully for a sound and it was then that I heard the slightest whimpering from upstairs. I moved to the bottom of the staircase again, wanting to get a better ear for it. It was coming from the main bedroom this time. Had Clara been in there all evening into these wee hours like I had? Too terrified to move, to even speak? Without even a thought, undoubtedly spirited and emboldened by the potent mixture of inebriation and delirium, I raced upstairs, moving towards the master bedroom. I could not leave my wife here, no matter how fearful I admit I was.

I swung the door open, bracing myself for whatever I might find inside, and shouted 'Clara!' but the room seemed empty. I hadn't even noticed but the whimpering I had heard had now stopped and the only noise I could hear was the dull thud-thud- thud of my quickening pulse, bulging rhythmically in the middle of my forehead, and my breath, or should I say panting, as I looked around. I looked towards the en-suite and the door was ever so slightly ajar, enough to show that the room was lit by the lamp. With infinitely more hesitance than I had shown by exploding into the main room, I pushed the door and quietly questioned,

'Clara?'

There was no stiffness in the door but it opened to reveal nobody or nothing inside. In that moment, I considered hiding and locking myself in there until morning, for the ostensible safety of light. I had not been afraid of the dark but now, with the shadows, the natural lack of light in the house, the noises that gave cause to question what I could not see, well, it did not cause me shame to confess I was frightened, frightened for my life. Even if what had happened to the first girl, Lauren, was nothing but a tragic accident, I could not... I did not, want to imagine the kind of horrors which faced her sister on these grounds. In that brief moment I almost felt reassured that if she had suffered in the same way, then death may have been a pleasant escape. Still, I considered, even if I was to seek solace in this small lit room, what good would waiting until light do me?

I was equally fearful of encountering the man again. Or seeing the woman, and her child, burning to death in front of my eyes. I kept being lured back. I had to break and leave and get as far away as possible. I had found no trace of Clara and I had to imagine, I had to believe that she had escaped.

These thoughts floated around my mind rapidly but I couldn't have been in the small room, held on to the door frame, for more than just a few seconds when I heard the voice of the boy again.

'Don't leave. Don't go, daddy.'

I closed my eyes. I hoped it would pass. I dare not look back into the room and so I brought myself to open my eyes and looked into the vanity mirror. I saw the boy sat on the bed with his back towards me, as if he were looking through the window.

'Jack,' I said. I didn't even ask. I knew.

He did not move.

I turned to face him and instead of Jack, or any boy, stood right in front of me, almost face to face, was the man who had stood facing me outside. Where once he had appeared weak and ill, he now seemed resolute, and far more intimidating than I could manage to be. He stared at me as if I were a trespasser on his land, as if I were about to suffer the same fate as others, a fate I now knew to be horrendous.

'No...'

I barely even managed to squeak the word out before my body convulsed violently, and whether by internal will or some external force my body was thrust against the bedroom wall. The man turned to face me, but I moved, able to generate some power in my limbs to get out of the room, able to escape before he could get near me. I could feel the cold and chill on the hairs of the back of my arms to my elbows and the rest of my body felt like it would be shuddering if I stopped for just a second.

As I left the room, at once, I heard the repeated banging on the door, the screaming, the crying, and this time, against the closed door, I could see a bright, burning orange illuminating the rim and glowing into the hallway. I could not stop.

I was able to move along the landing and down the stairs, and this time, I went straight to the kitchen and out through the doors on to the back. I stopped, briefly, holding the bricks at the side of my house to catch my breath.

'Clara! Clara if you're there, please shout!' I yelled in vain.

I did not want to leave without her. But I could not go back in there.

I stumbled to the front of the house, and out of it, and looked at the road at the tip of the hill's descent. I had every intention of racing to and down it without stopping but, compelled by the indecision to leave my wife, I turned back one last time. Stood in the main bedroom window, forbidding me from coming back into the house was the man. Whether it was Mr Argall, or the man who had built the house, I did not know. I did not wish to know.

I turned and ran and I didn't stop until I had reached the bottom.

Chapter Fifteen
Goodbye

I WAS undoubtedly powered by adrenalin but by the time I reached Dyffryn Du, my entire body was exhausted and I collapsed at the door of the White Horse. I was hysterical and, at one point, I felt as if I was not in my own skin, as if I were a spectator watching myself squirm on the floor.

I felt as if my knocks on the door were feeble but I must have been causing a commotion as I noticed lights come on, lights from the houses opposite. I dared not look up into the windows. Paul Appleton eventually came down and opened the door, looking down on me in the desperate state that I was. Our eyes met and so there was barely any need to converse.

'Clara... Clara... She's still there,' was all I could bring myself to say.

'Come on lad.'

Paul took me in and I must have passed out because I can't remember much of what happened for the rest of the night. Of what I do recall, Hector came and got me and took me out of Dyffryn Du, to the Percy Arms.

I was suffering sweats and panics and, for the next few nights, the most terrible nightmares I had ever endured. I kept thinking of going back to the house, or being in the house already and seeing Clara's body lit up in flames. In some I was father to Jack but he always had his back to me, or I was stood looking up at the window as the orange flames flickered, licked and decimated the bodies of my wife and child. I could feel the pain in those dreams as if I was his father, and the hopelessness and powerlessness that went with it. I felt as if I had let him down. In others I could just hear the foreshadowing of the furniture scrape. The agonised cry as the breath left the lungs.

These noises lived with me into my moments of consciousness and it became talk around Aberaernavon — and, I should definitely imagine Dyffryn Du too — that I had gone insane, or that the stories which had been whispered to them through generations were true, and that the man who owned Tŷ Glo — the Coal House — had once again sought revenge on someone foolish enough to attempt to occupy his house, someone so ill-considered to believe they could raise a family on those grounds. A family he didn't want, one he never wanted.

I waited for word on Clara but I was told the police visited Tŷ Glo and couldn't find a body. I knew. I knew they hadn't gone in. I could tell. I could not return and even if I had wanted to, I would have been stopped. I could not stand the prying eyes, sympathetic or judgemental, and in brief moments of clarity where I am sure I was still not thinking straight, I would prise myself away from my bed and out of the Percy Arms, and go to the library where I knew it would likely be quiet. I continued this routine for two or three days and I read books, books about anything, stories that would hopefully fill my head with other thoughts or distract me for any period of time.

The librarian would come and see if I was okay and I just

nodded, unable or unwilling to really converse. She understood. On one of the days she introduced me to a gentleman who said he was from the Aberaernavon Journal and would like to ask me a few questions. I remember telling him that my wife was there, so was the man, and that there was no doubt that the woman, Iris Argall, was real.

I wanted people to go to the house to rescue Clara even if just to get her body but knew that in good conscience I could not ask anyone. The newspaper ran the story and I came across like a lunatic — I heard the stories, I knew what people were saying, and in a matter of days it had become the story of choice the man had claimed the life of my wife and that Clara was now the woman who haunted the grounds of Tŷ Glo. Many of the people of the village grew too scared to talk to me or even approach me — save for Hector and Lillian — and, as I recovered, I began to wonder what my course of action would be.

Lillian's maternal instincts were at work and she was insistent that I remained with them for the duration of my convalescence though I had no diagnosable illness to speak of, nothing the doctors could say for sure. After doing the interview for the newspaper I began to come to terms with the likelihood that Clara had passed away, that something terrible had happened — what, exactly, I tried not to think of, but I knew that I had to begin the grieving process.

I felt a lot of guilt. Our last proper conversation had been about Clara having an abortion and I knew that she knew I was angry. It was difficult to live with that and so I began to write letters to her, telling her that I forgive her if there was anything to forgive, and that I was so sorry. I sent them to our old house in London and I would write and send one daily, firstly with those initial laments, then, later, I began to write of what I one day hoped would have become of us. Our life together back in London, away from all of this, and what might one day be. I found them to help although one day Hector caught me writing and saw that I had addressed the letter to Clara; he told me I was not doing myself any good in the long term. For me, it was all I could do to cope.

About two weeks passed of me sending these letters when I received a knock on my door saying there was some post for me. My heart skipped and my head inflated — Clara? Had she responded? Hector opened the door and passed me a bundle, a bundle of envelopes, all returned to me unopened. It was an awful blow and Hector sat with me for a while, neither of us saying anything.

My mood darkened for a while after that. Hector tried to galvanise me by saying I should do some work and he arranged to get me some work doing odds and ends for locals who he managed to convince that I wasn't totally crazy. So I would do bits around the house for elderly widowed ladies such as the replacement of shelves or repair of tables or floorboards. Hector, bless his heart, was trying to give me a purpose again, trying to get me back on my feet. He could only do so much and when it was time for me to finish work I would go back to my room and be alone, and drink, drink to escape my memories of the past and the present, to accelerate the evening so that I might wake up sooner, or to numb my memory so that for once I might not suffer a terrible nightmare.

The days were long, and it got so that I would give myself the excuse that once it got dark, I was allowed to begin to drink, and I would not stop. It made the days seem shorter and it dulled the pain, though, of course, waking with the grogginess and realisation that my problems were still there did nothing to help me in the long run. I was grateful to Hector and Lillian who showed tremendous patience with me but I was unable to speak to them. I knew in my heart that Lillian did not find it easy; after all, the state I was in must have been quite familiar to her, I imagined, but all that the guilt did from that was make me want to drink more. I was unable to confide in her and, as kind as they had been, I don't think that they would have wanted me to anyway.

On nights when I found myself unable to sleep, I continued to drink until it made me unconscious, and one time I felt compelled to write Clara another letter, expressing deep sorrow and regret of my own that I had been unable to save her. I did not attempt to articulate anything particularly well, I just wanted to pour my feelings out on to the paper, and as I wrote, I got angry, angry at the man, traumatised by the burning figure of Iris Argall, angry at myself for being so cowardly that I abandoned my wife — till death us do part, I must have wrote a hundred times, apologising for my failure to live to those vows. I sent that letter and felt it was quite cathartic, that I was channeling my anger in a better fashion, and so I wrote a number of these letters, addressed them to Tŷ Glo and posted them. Now, I am certain that no postman or postwoman would have dared to deliver them, but I felt a minute sense of liberation and that was enough for me to get through the day.

Now I had begun to dare to once more think of Tŷ Glo I had to wonder why, why me, why could this have all happened? Why did he appear to be prohibiting me from staying there? Why did I have to hear the screams, why did I have to see the burning bodies? Why did the boy call me Daddy? Was it out of spite or vengeance that he did whatever he had done to Clara? How much of the ghost of Iris Argall was something I should fear, or something I should pity and try to save? Did she seek to punish Clara for willingly giving up her child? I started to feel as if Clara had been a sacrifice. Was it the wish of these beings to drive me so insane that I believed I was Jack's father, once I had showed some sort of determination not to be scared away? I wondered about the story I had been told about the librarian and the picture I had seen in the house of the couple with the boy. Whatever, I was close to losing my mind on that evening, of that I was quite sure, and I established that this realisation and awareness must have been a positive sign as regards my own recovery.

Eventually I became more composed and, although I still carried around the heavy burden of grief and shock from what had been an unavoidably life-changing experience, the fear no longer dominated my thoughts, and I began to develop relationships, friendships, with the people of the village that I worked for, and I started to pay board for my keep with Hector and Lillian who were happy to keep me around.

I did not see or hear from the Appleton's, and, without wishing to sound uncaring of their own grief, that pleased me. I heard of the funerals of their girls and that made me approach the subject with Hector at dinner one evening.

I wondered if there was a way of holding a service to commemorate Clara even though her body had not been recovered and although I faced some initial resistance I was able to persuade the local church to hold a memorial for her. Just Lillian, Hector and I attended, but I felt it was a fitting thing to do and afterwards I was glad to have done it. I would continue to live with the events of what had happened over those few days, that night, forevermore, but I could now at least begin to look forward.

Now, I could never say that I had completely escaped the grief, but there comes a point where you naturally become less consumed with it, and that too was a process I managed to overcome. Still, I did not like the feeling of being alone, and even though my landlords were quite happy to have me around, they began to encourage me to perhaps take up a hobby, something that would get me out.

Unfortunately there was very little of note to do in Aberaernavon, save of walking or hiking in the nearby hills, and the isolation which accompanied it was not something I was prepared to deal with. I didn't know if I ever would be able to. I took to socialising down in the lounge and made a few acquaintances there, playing cards and such, but when the idea was suggested to join their local team, and go around to other public houses to play against darts teams, snooker teams and so on, I refused, as I still, ashamedly, felt fearful of traveling out in the dark. To say I was anxious and waiting for the lighter nights was an understatement.

Christmas had passed but I was still somewhat troubled at that point, yet to feel any better, and so it came and went without me so much as acknowledging it. Perhaps with the compassion that it would be a difficult day if I was aware of it, Lillian and Hector had treated it like any other day for me, not making any particular effort to change the norm. They just wanted me to be settled.

It was a different matter for my birthday in early February.

Lillian really went to an effort, baking me a cake and presenting me with a knitted jumper. I was touched — I really felt like I was part of the family and, to all intents and purposes, I may as well have been. I felt protected, even though, at the same time, I felt a little silly to feel this old and still feel like I needed to be protected. I had to act my age and be better than I had been. Rather than a day of celebration, it was a day to be pensive and reflect. Much like any other, I suppose. Though now, my contemplations turned to the future and for the first time since I had been to Tŷ Glo, I started to consider what my future might look like long term.

I could not stay at the Percy Arms forever. I did not want to even consider the prospect of going back to Dyffryn Du so I would just consider the house a write-off and start over. I had to seriously consider whether I wanted to remain in Aberaernavon, where I started to rebuild my life, or instead go back to London. It was not an obvious or easy decision to make. At least with this deliberation, I felt a little of the old me coming through, and that was a comfort. The rest of my birthday passed without event — I took the day off but did very little — and, I don't know if it was coincidence, but I slept well for the first time in forever.

When I woke up the following morning I had a greater sense of clarity and I felt ready to make a decision about what I would do with my life. I decided to go down to the churchyard and to the memorial plaque I had put on a plot in the graveyard. I talked to Clara, both in voice and in my head, asked her what I should do, asked her for some sign of what I ought to do with my life, where I ought to go. I waited, and there was silence, but a pleasant silence that was broken by birdsong. It was beautiful. I closed my eyes and tried to imagine that it was some message from Clara but, I knew it wasn't, however delightful and simple.

It was never pleasant leaving the memorial. I still felt as if I was leaving her again, abandoning her, and as I walked out of the graveyard I wondered if that in itself was a sign that I ought to stay in Aberaernavon, so that I could always be close by. I felt quite tearful for a short minute, wondering if I might always be plagued with this sadness.

I was to go back to work this morning and help Mrs Harris with her pantry shelves — she always made delicious, home-made scones and the anticipation of one put a spring in my step. Although the old dear made no secret of being happy for my company, sometimes I wondered who was benefitting more. I walked along the road back towards the Percy Arms to get my toolbox when something stopped me dead in my tracks.

A woman, getting out of a familiar car just outside the pub. A woman with the body shape from behind that was remarkably familiar. But it couldn't be. My blood ran cold and I shut my eyes tightly. I opened them again but the woman was still there, this time, fully out of the car — our other car — and straightening up her jacket.

'Clara,' I whispered, and then shouted. 'Clara?!'

My wife turned around and looked at me, clear as day. My stomach flipped and I instantly felt tears in my eyes. I held the wall that was beside the road for stability and crumpled on to it, unable to control my emotions, and Clara, very real indeed, came up and held me, comforting me and telling me everything was going to be alright.

Chapter Sixteen
The Hills

HECTOR AND Lillian were just as surprised to see Clara as I was and that first few minutes as we sat in the Percy Arms saw us all sat with some disbelief and Clara feeling shocked or stunned that we thought that she had died. Our hosts left us alone to talk privately.

Apparently, she had gone straight to London as soon as I had climbed into the bath, ashamed at what she had told me, and full of fear that I would leave her.

'I couldn't bear to see that look in your eye,' she said. 'And worse, know that it was my fault, that I deserved it. I didn't know if I could live with it.'

'There are things I need to tell you,' I said.

'And I you,' Clara attempted to interrupt.

'Please let me go first,' I said. 'I really, truly can't believe you are sat here in front of me. This is the best moment of my life.'

I began to get upset once more as I attempted to compose myself.

'We can do anything. Go anywhere. We can stay here, in the village. We can do whatever you want. I just want to be with you. But we can't go back to the house...'

Clara looked at me solemnly, as if she knew, she could read my eyes, and that she trusted in me. I was confident and stern rather than panicked and disturbed. Our grasp on each other's hands tightened.

'I can't believe that you thought I had died. What could have happened to make you believe that?' she enquired.

'I don't know where to begin. But it doesn't matter... I sent you letters. Letters, to London,' I remembered. 'But they came back to me.'

'Sorry. I'm sorry. I was so... I didn't believe you cared. I didn't want to read something that confirmed you were so angry with me,' she admitted. 'But then more came and I realised that you wouldn't have been angry, that wouldn't have motivated you to write all those letters, but if was forgiveness, then I felt I deserved that even less, and I was too ashamed to open them after running away. I didn't want to throw them away and so I sent them back.'

'I thought... Never mind, you're here,' I said. 'And I couldn't be happier. But if you felt that way, then why, why are you here?'

Clara held my hand tighter.

'I'm pregnant,' she whispered. 'Four months.'

'What?' I could barely believe my ears. 'But, how?'

'I don't know. I really don't. It's a miracle,' she said. 'I found out last week and I just had to tell you... I started to come up yesterday because I wanted to surprise you on your birthday but I felt tired on the journey so had to stop and sleep. There was a nice little bed and breakfast, just outside of Gloucester in the Cotswolds.'

'You could have called.'

'Some things are better said face to face.'

'Some things,' I said with a beaming smile on my face, ignorant of the tears which decorated it, 'are fated.' Clara smiled and then laughed.

We told Hector and Lillian of our news and of course, they being the wonderful hosts we had become accustomed to, Lillian declared it a celebration and made a huge brunch with champagne to add. It was only just opening time at the pub but Hector declared that drinks were on the house and so it soon got full for a weekday morning. Even Mrs Harris came in — with all that went on, I had completely forgotten about her pantry, but she was quick to forgive me once she learned of my wonderful news and a glass of sherry was put in her hand.

Even though Clara barely knew any of the villagers, they knew me, and knew of my loss... or, what I had thought was my loss... and were genuinely pleased and delighted for me. She was treated like a long lost friend. At numerous times through the morning and early afternoon both of us were brought to tears, sometimes by something one of us said, sometimes just by the moment.

I'm not sure that Clara truly appreciated or acknowledged the fact that I honestly had thought that she had passed away as the victim of some violent act or accident. Or that I, myself, had carried around this guilt which I now realised was misplaced but still could not magically turn off. For her, she had come back, and given me the most incredible news, and while it was all that, I was so overwhelmed that I had to make my excuses and go to the bedroom for a while. Clara followed.

'Are you okay?' she closed the door behind her.

'Yes... I just think, maybe the champagne has gone to my

head,' I said. She sat down beside me and we just held each other and wept.

'I am happy. Really, I am,' I managed to say after a while composing myself. 'I could not happier. It's just... everything. I didn't expect it.'

'I know it's a lot to take in. Perhaps we should go for a walk,' Clara smiled. 'Get away from it all and talk.'

I thought it was a great idea. We managed to sneak out unnoticed down the stairs and through the front door, so as not to disturb such a jovial atmosphere or, more pertinently, be dragged back into it.

We walked through the village, aimlessly really, but with our familiar path of direction taking us to the hills.

'What would you like to do... where would you like to live?' asked Clara. 'Honestly, I'll be happy with you, wherever, but it's up to you, wherever you think you will be happy.'

'Well, what do you think?' I asked back. I didn't want to be selfish and come to a decision without her.

'You do appear to have grown quite attached to these people... it would be quite nice to have a family. They seem like a family,' she said.

'Yes... yes, I suppose they are. Funny, I'd never really thought of it like that, but that has certainly been the case as of late. They have done a lot for me,' I admitted.

'I was lonely back in London. I know that if you were there it would be less so but... oh, wouldn't it be nice to have family around. To have people around our child,' she replied.

'Our child,' I squeezed her hand tighter. 'I still can't believe it. I still can't. It really is a miracle... Yes, I guess we could stay here. We could.'

We walked, carefully, up into the hills, and sat for some time gazing out over the landscape. I had been there before and felt its isolation but now, with chatter in my ear — Clara found it most amusing that I had become a handyman for the local villagers, joking that she would have to learn to share me with all the mother hens — its true beauty was restored and appeared to solidify our decision to stay.

A silence followed, where we just enjoyed each other's company once more. I reasoned that Clara might not ever understand what it was to grieve in the way that I had but at the same time, I felt as if telling her would serve no purpose at all. I hoped she would never have to feel the way I did so why should I explain to her exactly how it was?

That silence was broken by Clara.

'You know, I have a feeling it will be a boy,' she said.

I smiled, and thought.

'A son? That would be nice. But I will be happy... No, I will be thrilled whatever we have. I just pray for a healthy baby. And a healthy wife of course,' I said, wrapping my arm around her tighter.

Later, we made our way back to the Percy Arms, where the party in our honour had died down and everything seemed back to normal. Normal. It felt good to feel that way again.

We had an evening meal with Hector and Lillian, telling them of our plans to stay in the village and Clara was racing away with ideas of where she would like to stay and how she would like to decorate. It was typical of her, and so re-assuring. It had been a long time — even before we came to the village — since I had seen a natural vibrancy from her and I really felt that being expectant seemed to bring out the best in her. She looked good, beautiful, perfect, and I had fallen in love with her all over again. I had put any change in attitude that she may have had down to the death of our parents happening in a fairly short space of time but now I knew that some of what had hardened her was her own personal trouble. Now she had come back into my life, any negative thought or feeling I had originally held had vanished and was instantly dampened by the remembrance of the grief I had already gone through. My life was nothing without her — I could have carried on but I was not the same person... nothing remotely negative needed to be carried through to this life, this new life, that we were going to share together.

It was quite a day and I had felt a tremendous exhaustion at the end of it. I was exhilarated but tired; but when my head hit the pillow, I was unable to get any sleep whatsoever. I tried to talk to Clara but she fell asleep quite soon and I didn't want to disturb her. I began to entertain the thought of being a father, and it was tremendously exciting, because I had effectively completely ruled out the prospect of anything like that ever happening. Not just because of what had happened with Clara, but even if she had... if she had not come back, then as I was, I could not see me finding love again, and even if I did, with a local, I would have felt a sense of responsibility not to have a child.

It was a curious logic and one I didn't fully understand. I don't know if I felt the curse of Tŷ Glo weigh heavy on me, if that was my cross to bear, if I ought to be a martyr to it. I was still trying to work through those thoughts as it was, before Clara's return, and those 'why me's circled in my head once more, only now, in a good way. I felt truly blessed.

I noted my over-thinking getting the better of me again and so I closed my eyes and tried to let all thoughts flow out, bring in the emptiness, and just feel nothing, and think nothing.

For a time, I could hear nothing, and I think I had gone past the point of exhaustion, when I begun to hear something. The sound of a chair being dragged along the hallway outside the room.

I became frozen with fear, as the sound was identical to the one I heard time and time over in Tŷ Glo, the sound of the scratching of furniture against the wooden floor. Then it stopped. And the silence was the worst of all. I don't know why, but after it stopped, I expected to hear the banging, the cries, and I waited, and waited. I couldn't tell if it was my imagination or maybe Hector had taken to moving things around in the middle of the night — he was always doing something — but I could not hear footsteps so I ruled out the latter. I thought I was being silly, hyper-sensitive, as if my conscious had decided I needed something to worry about, but every time I felt I was drifting off in to sleep, there it was again, the scratching, along the floor outside, and then stopping, with the loaded pause. It constantly kept me awake.

I cannot explain how these things happen but Clara must have sensed my restlessness and woke.

'Are you okay?'

'I just thought I heard something... I'm okay.'

'Are you sure?'

I nodded.

'Go to sleep, Finn.'

Under Clara's watchful eye, I was able to drift off into sleep.

CHAPTER SEVENTEEN
Snow

WHEN I woke in the morning I instantly wondered if I had enjoyed the most wonderful dream. This feeling grew when I turned over and where I imagined Clara had been laid, she was in fact not. I moved over and smelled her pillow and was comforted by it — it had not been a dream, it was quite real. I came around and waited for a few moments, wondering if she was in the bathroom.

'Clara?' I asked, but received no reply.

I went downstairs and into the kitchen where Lillian and Hector were enjoying their breakfast. We exchanged our morning pleasantries.

'What do you expect to do today?' asked Lillian.

'Well I must tend to Mrs Harris' pantry, or she might begin to get cross with me, and I can't have that,' I joked. 'But before that I wanted to make sure what Clara was doing. Or, I wanted to. Has she been down?'

'Yes, she had some toast but has already gone out. She said she would go for a walk. About twenty minutes or so, she hasn't been long.'

'Okay.'

'Would you like some toast?' asked Lillian.

'No, I'm okay; I might go and see where Clara is. It looks nice out,' I said.

'Yes, but its cold, lad. Reckon it's going to snow, they say. I've been out there a while this morning moving the crates and it's brisk. You'll catch your death,' said Hector.

'Right... I'll wrap up,' I assured him.

I went back upstairs and got dressed and ready. It's silly but I almost didn't want to be apart from Clara, as if there was so much lost time to make up for, as if we didn't have the rest of our lives in front of us. But, I guessed that was at least a good thing, and tried to feel that it wasn't an indication of me being scared of being alone again. At once, I felt a bit foolish about the previous night, about being fearful of the sounds of the house, for that must have been all it could have been. Everything was fine, now.

I went downstairs and was force-fed some toast by Lillian who refused to allow me to leave the house without it and as she passed it to me, the plate was held on a short stack of papers and she said,

'Oh, Clara left these down here yesterday, well, I think they are yours... I didn't take to looking at them.'

Sure enough, they were — as I ate, I fingered through the documents, house deeds, insurance papers — I couldn't quite figure out what exactly I was reading, but, it did seem as if she had already sold our property. Her birth certificate was there — I smiled as I began to realise that she was serious about moving here. And, in that moment, it wasn't so much where we were, as it was the commitment to me, which made me feel so wonderful.

I was about to stand up and make my move to go outside when I couldn't help but flick to my own birth certificate. It occurred to me that I had never even seen it before — I hadn't had cause to, as I had inherited the house I had grown up in, and Clara had always dealt with all of the family paperwork. At first, my eyes couldn't quite comprehend what they were seeing. I flicked past it at first, scrolling past the paper, looking for others, but there were none. It must have been mine.

'Jack Howell' it read, born February 5th, 1925, Aberaernavon, North Wales.

Lillian could tell I was spooked.

'What is it, boy?' she asked, softly.

'This...' I passed it to her.

She took the paper and quickly sat down. Her knees must have felt just as weak as mine.

There was a period of silence. I could not understand it, any of it. I looked at the paper for some time before looking up and noticing that Lillian's eyes were fixed on mine. She placed her hands on mine, her just as cold as mine.

'It's me. But how...?'

'You...'

We both, again, sat silent for a few moments.

'A few years after the war, I don't know, two or three,' she started. 'A young family moved up there. And there was... an accident pretty quickly.'

'A fire.'

'An accident,' she insisted. 'And the mother died. But the boy, he was saved, and sent away.'

'I am struggling to understand, to make sense of any of this, surely I should remember.'

'The boy was only two or three. You wouldn't.'

Quietly, I began to think. Everything was so familiar. But it couldn't explain the ghosts, the people.

'But, Iris Argall... why me?'

'Pardon?'

'I am certain about the ghosts, I have seen them,' I continued, but, before I could go on, Hector came over to our table and interrupted.

'I think we should stop here, Lillian.'

I looked at her and only then realised how upset she had become.

'Give it a while, boy,' Hector said.

Uneasily, I stood, and decided that I ought to go and find Clara, to talk to her, and maybe we could try and understand together. Did she know about the birth certificate?

The cold hit me hard. It was one of those dry but bitterly cold and slightly windy mornings, where the ground was almost preparing to accept a heavy snowfall. Hector's information about the weather certainly seemed spot on. We had not yet had snow over the winter and while that sort of weather would cause chaos in London's busy streets, up here, where life was slower and the place was a lot smaller, I had almost felt the excitement and anticipation of a young child, waiting for it to fall.

The village had plenty of charm as it was and the idea of snow covering the scenery, providing a pure canvas of white, I imagined that Clara would be up on the hill, hoping to see snow fall and witness some of it.

I was, of course, rather distracted by my discovery. Peculiarly, I was not struck by the thought or worry of being adopted, or even the life I had led with not knowing my roots, but more, haunted by a feeling that all of this was beginning to make sense. Suddenly, the air of familiarity was logical. I was keen to learn more about what had happened, but I was able to determine from the words that were not said that if I was in fact from a family that had been in the Coal House, they had suffered the same fate as others before. And I could deduct from that, the man I had seen on a number of occasions, the man who nobody could describe or tell me the identity of, could be my own father. The woman was not Iris Argall at all, but my own mother, my real mother. In a very strange way, I felt some relief, some connection, and felt a purpose to inform Clara as soon as possible.

I walked rather swiftly along the roads towards the hills and snow did indeed begin to fall and quite heavily, settling on the ground. It quickened my pace and once I got to the small pathway that led there I had the strangest feeling, I don't know if it was an aroma, the natural scent of my wife which I recognised, but I just knew I was following where she had walked. It made me smile widely, a smile of comfort rather than joy, and put a real spring in my step. I walked past some trees to the clearing of the ascent up the hill, which was now quickly becoming covered in a thin white blanket, and I snaked around one of the rickety, uncertain bends, until Clara began to come into view, sat quite high on one of the many stones which provided an impromptu seat.

'Clara!' I called, with delight in my voice.

She turned and smiled at me and shouted back.

'It's beautiful, isn't it!'

I smiled and moved forward, moving slightly around the curve of the hill.

Suddenly, my blood ran cold and I stopped still.

Stood further back, revealed by my walk up the hill, was the man from the land which surrounded our house, the man who I had reckoned to be my father. He looked at me, and I him, and it was not the glance of a man who held any love, or affection whatsoever, for me. My eyes quickly moved to Clara, and not out of fear for looking at the man, but fear for my wife. Between them, the petroleum mist I had come to dread began to materialise, and within it, the figure of a woman began to form. It caught my eye, dragging it away from Clara for a second, as I noticed a kindly expression — yet, when the form became more real, as real as the man, the expression changed to anguish, and the burns and blisters began to appear on her skin, causing the figure to scream. I could not bear to look and looked back at my wife.

Clara could not have seen either of them because she seemed blissfully unaware and as she looked back at me a look of concern washed over her face for what I must have looked like. She stood, I suppose to come towards me, but I knew, I knew what was about to happen and I tried to get the words out as soon as I could.

'Clara, don't. No...'

'What?' she just about managed to say, before she lost her footing on the unstable pathway and slipped. I was too far away to try and catch her. Too far away from her to do anything but watch her tumble, uncontrollably down the hill, over and over herself, only coming to a stop when she was forced to by a huge boulder, on which she banged her head.

The entire time I felt as if I were watching a moving picture, as if it weren't real, but I felt eyes on me, vengeful eyes of the man, I could feel the sneer and the hateful glee, but when I turned my head back up, with every intention of running up to this man and attacking him myself, to hell with the consequences, he had gone, disappeared from the backdrop of the purest white against which he had stood so boldly and prominently. The air was as clear as it could be.

I raced up to where he had stood and looked around but could see no-one.

And then I looked down to my wife. Clara was motionless against the rock and so I careered down the hill to get by her side. I knew that it was too late, too late to save her, but I had to go to her.

From the way she had struck the rock and was laid against it her face looked rather peaceful and I dare not turn her head to see otherwise. I cradled her body in my arms, weeping, before I realised I had a tough decision to make. I had to leave her to see if there was any chance of our baby being saved, and so I rushed back into the village, frantically telling the first person I could find, a passer-by, to call an ambulance, and to go to the Percy Arms and tell them.

I must have sounded hysterical but I was not in control of my senses, I just had to rush back to be with Clara, and when I returned to her, her dormant body was becoming covered by the snow, with blood reddening the white around her.

I sat there with her until the ambulance men came but I did not need to be told what had happened, that I had lost my wife for good, and our unborn child. He had done what he needed to do and truly took the only things that mattered to me. I was alone.

I closed my eyes and just wished, hoped and prayed that I would not be able to open them again.

EPILOGUE

I WRITE this letter to anyone whom it may concern.

Since the death of my wife, Clara, I have been unable to live with myself.

I am unable to live with the guilt of her passing. Of the death of my unborn child. Or the deaths of the young daughters of the Appleton family. I apologise to the people of Dyffryn Du and those aware of the story of Tŷ Glo — the Coal House — and the presence of the ghosts that haunted the land. I did not believe and I should have. I did not know. I am not directly to blame for the loss of these loved ones but I have been to Tŷ Glo and I have seen everything. I apologise for the part my family played before I was old enough to realise, and for the part I played when I was.

For anyone reading this letter and wondering if the stories and legends are true, then I have to tell you that they are, and I have suffered the most terrible consequences, consequences I shall live with for the rest of my days, consequences I feel responsible for.

I am the legal owner of Tŷ Glo and I hereby forbid trespassers on my estate. This is my cross to bear. I have not seen the ghosts since my wife was taken and I do not expect to because they have taken their awful revenge on me. I carry the burden of martyrdom on me now and will inhabit the land.

For the good of the people I implore that anyone with the sense of responsibility continue to share this message in no uncertain terms.

Do not try to find me. Do not try to save me. Tell all who ask, all who need to know, to never come to Tŷ Glo.

ACKNOWLEDGEMENTS

Thanks to Karen Butler for all her patience, enthusiasm and support. A profound thank you to David Lonsdale and to Carole Summers Ruffner for their eyes and feedback in the creation process. Sincere thanks to Charles Baker. Special thanks to Ash Temple and Karen Ronan for their outstanding creative minds in bringing my words to life. Thank you to my always patient and ever encouraging wife Stacey, my mum and Wes for their ideas and input.